What I am looking for is not out there, it is in me.
Helen Keller

About the author

Pauline Burgess is a writer and teacher from County Down who is inspired every single day by the children around her, including her daughter and her students. The Arts Council of Northern Ireland recognised her passion for writing for children when they granted her the Artists' Career Enhancement Award in 2013. Her series for younger readers – *Pony Friends Forever* – has become extremely popular with primary schools all over Northern Ireland, and *Pony Surprise* was an Eason top-ten bestseller. Pauline regularly visits schools and libraries across Ireland in her capacity as an author and active proponent of reading for pleasure.

Acknowledgements

Firstly, a big thank-you to the team at Poolbeg who saw the potential in *Knock Back* and walked me through each stage of its editing and publication. You made me and my story feel so welcome, right from the beginning. A very special thank-you to Gaye Shortland for her astute observations.

To my family and friends who have supported me through thick and thin, and especially to Paul and Emma who have lived through the highs and lows of every story I've written. And to Mum and Dad who always knew how much I wanted to write stories.

To my friends in the writing world who've stimulated, consoled and galvanised me in equal measure.

To my colleagues and students who have watched me go from teacher to teacher/writer and inspired me along the way. (I won't mention which student's pet inspired Sindy the Corn Snake.)

And, finally, to all the writers who have inspired my love of children's and teenage fiction. I am thankful to all the authors who have made my life easier as a teacher. I cannot name them all, but a special thanks to Joan Lingard who was brave enough to write about teenagers in Northern Ireland when no-one else did. Thank you.

Dedication

For Paul, who has supported me through all the *knock backs*.

Prologue

You can't really exist in this world without leaving a little bit of something behind: school reports, Facebook posts, texts, letters from school about 'unacceptable behaviour'. All kinds of stuff. And scars too. I have a thin white line next to my left eye that no-one's ever explained. And a recurring nightmare about a pitch-black night, metal crushing, a woman screaming. Dad's advice is not to overthink it. That's Dad all over: why complicate things by thinking about them? Mum's the total opposite. She's from the 'We need to talk about this' camp – all metaphors and profound sayings. Seriously, I can't decide which of them bugs me the most. That's partly why I decided to go. I really needed some space and I *really* needed some answers. Funny thing is, I ended up with answers to questions I'd never even asked.

Chapter one

So, there we were, driving along these narrow, country roads to Knockmore Farm – this special place in the countryside that treats kids like me. I had read that it was a place that helped *'families in crisis'*, but my family wasn't in crisis. Apparently, it was just me that was the problem. And, of course, good old Mum and Dad looked on the bright side and said it was all for the best.

'You'll love it, Ben – living and working on a farm for the summer. Taking care of horses, chickens, cows …You'll get a new perspective, love.'

Whatever that meant! All I could imagine was chicken-shit and cattle-muck, but if that's where they wanted to send me, then bring it on! After all, it was my idea in the first place. Dad hadn't actually found that page in the *Belfast Telegraph* by himself. I'd put it there on the coffee table right in front of the TV, exactly on the spot where he'd put his feet up and watch Man City. '**Knockmore Farm – A Residential Centre for Helping Teenagers Build Self-esteem.**' Mum's social-worker mate had told me about it. But I wasn't interested in building anything. All I wanted to do was to find out the truth and if it meant looking at bovine mammals for twelve hours a day, then so be it!

I did my best to look peeved about it and locked myself in my room for a few hours. I felt bad about upsetting Amy, though. She was only seven and still thought I was God's gift. I really hadn't *meant* to trample her corn snake, but when she saw the squishy remains of Sindy the Snake she nearly screamed the house down, and she was even worse when she heard I was going to be sent away over it.

'*He didn't mean it, Mum! It was an accident!*' she had shrieked down the stairs.

Her wee hands were covered in snake-guts and I just knew she would have tried to hide the whole mess if it wasn't for Mum finding her hovering over Sindy's corpse.

'For God's sake, Ben! *What* were you thinking of?' Mum rolled her eyes to the high heavens for maybe the tenth time that day. '*Why* did you take her out of her tank in the first place? And then prance about and end up trampling her?'

What could I say? That I was Saint Patrick the Second? Nah, I just shook my head and retreated, letting Mum and Dad jump to conclusions and decide on my fate. They must have stayed up until after midnight talking in, like, *really* loud whispers. I could hear Dad complain about my deteriorating behaviour and Mum saying it was just 'a call for attention'.

Amy cheered up a bit though when I told her that Sindy had gone to Snake Heaven: a sort of paradise of coiled snakes slithering away to their scales' content. She loved the idea that they might drop down from there: millions of snakes falling from the sky while people did their shopping – or sat on the bog – or whatever. She has a BIG imagination, my wee sister!

I spent the evening before my departure trying to pack for my Bear Grylls experience at Knockmore. Trouble was, I hadn't a clue what I'd need. I didn't even *own* a pair of wellies – well, you don't have much need for rubber boots in the suburbs. I packed a few T-shirts and jeans and stuff and then spent about half an hour wondering whether I'd need a torch or matches or, you know, survival kind of gear.

I could be sleeping under the stars for all I knew! I took a look at my clean, comfy bed in my not-so-clean, comfy room and wondered when I'd next have a decent night's sleep. Our house was on a tree-lined avenue – no bellowing bulls or crowing cockerels to wake you at an unearthly hour. No tractors thrumming past your window when you're trying to sleep through your alarm. The noisiest thing on Chester Road was probably my mum's dolphin music!

'Ben? Can I come in?'

It was Mum's Guilty Voice – the one she uses when she thinks she's failed as a parent. Without waiting for an answer, she came in and sat down on the edge of my bed. She started picking through my holdall and I noticed the lines on her forehead crease up when she saw the box of matches.

'Well, there mightn't be any electricity. How am I supposed to know what I need?' I grumbled. Then I realised she thought I had a more sinister use for them in mind. Well, there *was* my chip-pan experiment in the back garden that had gone slightly wrong … 'Crikey, Mum, what do you think I am? A flippin' arsonist?'

'Please don't swear, Ben. You know I don't think that. I just … I just wasn't sure why you were taking them. Listen, there's every convenience at

Knockmore, *including* electric lights, so I can safely say you can leave the matches at home. Now, how are you feeling about all this? About Knockmore?'

'How do you think I'm feeling?' I answered, without looking at her. 'I'm thinking you and Dad reckon I'm a delinquent and you can't wait to see the back of me for two months.'

I could hear the sigh, the long, slow release of breath that said I was being unreasonable – *again* – and that they were at their wits' end about me – *again!* But I wasn't going to make it easy on them, even if I did have my own agenda at the funny farm. Part of me felt guilty for hurting her like this. Part of me hated her for twelve years of lies.

She stopped speaking after that and left me to it. She didn't say a word to me this morning either, and the journey to Knockmore felt like a funeral. Nobody, I mean *nobody* spoke.

Belfast streets gave way to these windy roads that should have been off-road tracks, and the way Dad was driving I thought I was going to have to get out and *push* the car! Mum kept looking round at me with these big sad eyes but Dad didn't flinch. He stared straight at that road ahead because there was just *no way* he was going to take a wrong turn – he was taking me to Knockmore by hook or by crook, even if it took all day to get there. Apparently he'd had enough of my smart-ass personality of late and seriously believed that Knockmore was going to bring his son back. Whatever!

Then we came over a hill and I saw Strangford Lough loom up below us like a big puddle, with little islands splattered through the middle of it. And it was actually quite cool. I thought I could see these grey seals bobbing on the shoreline and part of me started to feel good about this whole thing. But then I looked at Amy – her chin was doubled on her chest and her lips were pouting like a goldfish – and I started to have second thoughts. All I had to do was say sorry and promise to make an effort and I knew Mum would have Dad turn the car round faster than a Ferrari. Well, a Ford Focus in our case. But I wouldn't do that. There was way too much at stake.

Down the hill we went and then started to climb steadily again. Then, following a sign, we turned in through a big pillared gate and up a long driveway, still climbing gradually, until we came to a stop in front of a big country-house type building, with a modern, glass-panelled, glitzy bit attached.

I could feel the sea breathing on me as soon as I opened the car door. A plane, probably an Easyjet fifty-five hours behind schedule, drew a thin white line across the sky. Mum was watching the lough swelling below and I just knew she was going to go all bloody philosophical on me. Well, at least she was speaking to me again.

'You know, this is a time to grow, Ben.' She breathed out. 'And a time to reap what you sow.'

Seriously – I could *not* handle another farming metaphor! She'd been coming out with them for over a week now – apparently my stay here would 'bear fruit' and allow my 'fertile imagination' time to mature. After a while I couldn't even hear them – they'd become like white noise – but now they were getting to me again.

'Look at this place! It's paradise, Ben. You'll be a man when you leave here!'

Technically, no – I would still be a teenager, but I let that one pass. She'd been in a funny mood ever since I was signed up for this place, convincing herself that it was the right thing to do. Poor Mum – she was always looking for 'solutions' – but hey, sometimes you just couldn't fix things. She pushed her hand through her hair and sighed like it was going to be her last breath.

Me, I was still focusing on the waves below us and thinking about throwing off my trainers and letting the water cut into my skin. But I was no Water Baby – that was Amy. She was the one who would love splashing about in the lough, feeling the white tips of spray against her shins. But Amy just stood there, with her hair all over her face, the colour of a blackbird.

Dad, though, he was already hauling my suitcase out of the car and striding across to the 'Knockmore Farm Reception' in the glitzy part.

Right enough, the place didn't look like a lunatic asylum – more like one of those country spa houses Mum went to when she needed 'Me Time' – part olde worlde, part modern chic. But I wasn't going to be taken in that easily. They probably had sweatshops out the back and torture chambers for snake-squishers.

'Therapeutic Learning Environment', it said across the top of the reception desk. A woman with short bobbed hair and a name badge that said Kate Bridges was beaming at us from behind the desk. She made a brief welcome speech and Dad signed a few papers. Then Kate Bridges confiscated my mobile phone, smarmily explaining that no phones were allowed 'for the duration'. Crap. I hadn't expected that.

Dad looked around the place, nodding his head as if he had found Nirvana. He scanned all the phrases that zig-zagged around the walls: Positive Behaviour, Mutual Respect, Self-discipline. Then he looked at me like he was going to deliver a Dad

Lecture, his eyes all piercing and serious, so I asked Kate where the nearest bog was and took off upstairs.

I could see fields that went on forever through a large window at the top of the stairs and there were three or four horses down below me in one of them. I stood there, watching their mouths munching on grass as if they didn't have a care in the world, breath steaming from them. Then I noticed some two-storey modern buildings that looked like classrooms at the back of the main building. Great! So *that's* where the punishment would begin!

When I went back downstairs Dad and Kate Bridges were gone. I had a nosy round. There was a large kitchen to the back of reception, which I thought an odd place to have one. Probably the kitchen in the main house was too old-fashioned – in the basement maybe, like a lot of them were in the old days. A few people were busying themselves cooking but they didn't see me taking a sneak peek.

'Ben? Are you there? Come on, son – Mr Wilson's waiting to talk to us.'

Dad again. All grave and commanding.

Wilson was the owner of Knockmore House and director of the 'troubled teens' programme – which was funded by all sorts of benefactors and grants of course.

I followed Dad along the hallway that joined the glitzy part to the main house and then to a big room with a huge, dark, round wooden table in the centre.

Mr Wilson (in a suit), Kate Bridges and another woman were sitting there, smiling at me as if my lights were on but there was nobody in. Amy and Mum were already beside them.

'Hello, Ben.' Wilson waved a hand, indicating that we should sit down.

We sat.

'I'm John Wilson. This is Allie Cooper our farm manager – you've already met Kate Bridges our admissions officer.'

Kate and John the Head Honcho still had smiles pasted on their faces – but it was Allie Cooper who seemed to really focus on me and take me in. I felt her eyes puncture mine like she was searching for something, so I searched right back. Her eyes were a kind of hazel – goldy-green – but I looked so hard I could see these little brown speckles in them. Like a song thrush. Weird!

'Ben, would you like to tell us why you're here?' asked the Head Honcho, twitching his monobrow which crawled across his forehead like a caterpillar.

'Because I squished a snake?'

'Well, it wasn't just that, Ben. There were, em, *other* incidents too, weren't there?' he said, still smiling.

'Ye…es,' I answered. Bloody hell, did he want me to list them?

Dad shook his head as if he wished the ground would swallow him up.

'But we're not interested in going through a litany of your offences today, Ben – we're interested in talking about how we can change things.' The Honcho shook his head repeatedly.

I was afraid if he kept doing it his comb-over would flop back over. And I did *not* want to see that.

I was relieved that we didn't have to go through my *litany of offences* because I couldn't remember half of them anyway. Crashing into a hearse on my bike, peeing into the Guides' campfire, that chippan experiment – I could remember those at least. The thing is, I wasn't a *bad* lad, just a lad who screwed up a lot – but I had to screw up, because it was the only way to get to Knockmore.

After nearly half an hour of pep talk, the Honcho walked Mum and Dad out. Me and Amy followed. Mum looked like she'd changed her mind about the whole thing but Dad was sticking to his guns.

'He has to do it, Claire. He has to find himself.'

Huh – now *that* was ironic! *Find* myself?

I rolled my eyes and let them say their goodbyes: Mum all weepy and perfumey and Dad straight as a single 4-iron. Then I squeezed Amy's hand and made her promise not to hate me.

'I'll buy you new snakes, Ames, I promise. Big fat scary ones – just the way you like them, okay?'

'Poisonous?' she asked hopefully, her blue eyes peeking at me from under her flap of a fringe.

'Maybe not, Ames, just to be on the safe side. Come and see me, though. Okay?'

''Kay.'

The car drove off. Amy waved from the back seat and I thought I saw Mum dabbing at her eyes in the mirror. Dad looked straight ahead. I stood there and watched the car crinkling the air and shining on the long driveway of Knockmore.

Two months. I had just two months to find out everything I needed to know. Either I was completely freakin' bonkers for coming here or I was on the cusp of the biggest discovery of my life. There was only one way to find out and I had the strangest feeling something or someone was waiting for me, right here at Knockmore.

Chapter two

'You're in Block C, Ben, right over there,' said the Head Honcho. 'Room 11. Do you need someone to walk you over, or are you happy enough to sort yourself out?'

'I *think* I can manage,' I said.

'Good,' he nodded. 'We have four rooms in the old house but they're used for long-term residents.' He winced as he said 'long-term'. 'You're out on the new section because we're sure you won't be here for long, Ben.'

And he gave me a smile that was somewhere between a grimace, a sneeze and a snarl. This guy was a weirdo. And who the hell named a place Block C? Just ten minutes ago the Honcho had told me *not* to think of this place as a prison.

I walked past some stables where a couple of lads were shovelling what looked like hay. Whatever it was, it was absolutely bloody minging!

The door to Block C was open so I ploughed on up the stairs to Room 11 and was surprised to find I had the room to myself. I guess I shouldn't have been – there were only sixteen inmates, the Honcho said. A single bed, a desk and chair, and a view across the farm. It was practically a Premier Inn!

I threw myself down on the bed and thought I'd have myself a nap or maybe even have a nosey about and find the rest of the inmates.

A quick hard knock and the door opened. No privacy here then.

I looked at the guy standing in the doorway. Staff obviously.

'Ben Parker?'

'Yeah?'

'I'm Jack. You want to come with me and I'll show you what duty you're on this afternoon?'

'No, thanks. I'm alright, Jack.'

'I'm glad you're *alright*, Ben, I'm delighted to hear it in fact, but you're still coming with me.'

So, they used sarcasm in this 'special' place? Why did he make it sound like an invitation when it was an order in the first place then? This Jack guy's hair was so skinhead short he looked like a bloody marine or something. I was just dying to put him in the picture and tell him that he was taking the whole Boot Camp look a bit far, what with his skintight T-shirt and bulging biceps.

'You're on horticulture today so you're going to plant some tomatoes, cucumbers, that kind of thing!' he called back, marching off down the corridor.

'Why?' I asked.

He turned back to face me. 'Why? *Why*? Would you like to eat while you're here, Ben?'

His face was beginning to twist into what I was beginning to recognise as the Knockmore Smile.

'I assumed you'd just, like, go to Tesco's – or something?'

'And where would the learning experience be in that, Ben? *Hmm*? You need to plant, to nurture, to watch, to grow.' He stood rooted to the corridor, looking like a bloody gym instructor. 'These things will teach you about productivity as well as self-regard. Farming isn't just nourishment for the body, but for the soul.'

Uh-oh! The words *funny* and *farm* were creeping into my head again. Maybe I hadn't actually done enough homework on this place. I decided to humour the bloke though.

'Okay, Jack,' I said slowly. 'Tomatoes and cucumbers it is then.'

I swear I saw a crease in his brow. Weren't these guys supposed to stay calm and tolerant at all times?

'Come on then. You're on with Heath.'

Heath turned out to be short for Heathcliff. *Seriously*! We'd just finished a book in school about this moody bloke who moped about on the moors and now here I was in some parallel Emily Brontë universe with another moody bloke who literally didn't speak. *Ever*!

'Heath chooses not to communicate with the world except through gestures,' Jack the Lad explained, before handing me a shovel and leaving me to it.

Great!

'Er, hiya,' I said to Silent Boy.

He looked about two or three years older than me. Tall and tanned and sort of broody-looking, with a lot of hair and a big floppy fringe across his eyes. And headphones around his neck.

Silent Boy said nothing.

'So, what do I do?' I asked him.

No response.

There was a scattering of small plants lying on the ground so I supposed I was meant to, well, *plant* them.

18

'Just stick these in the ground then?' I asked.

Still no response. He nodded towards a bucket of muck or compost or something, handed me a rake, pointed to a spot and disappeared. Friggin' hell, didn't anybody give any lessons around here before, like, throwing you in at the deep end? I started pointlessly raking at the soil and was beginning to wish Amy's corn snake was still hissing in its tank. Then Silent Boy came back with a watering can and nodded at me like I knew what I was doing. Actually I did, after a while. I just copied him and before I knew it there were three rows of tomato plants in the ground.

'Not bad, Heath?' I said, pointing at my work. 'Are we done?'

It was actually getting pretty hot out here so I reckoned a can of Coke and a rest were well deserved.

Silent Boy had his headphones on so I hoped he could lip-read.

Apparently he could. He looked at me like I was a sandwich short of a picnic and shook his hair, then pointed at a pack of seeds. Cucumber seeds. He placed his hands about twenty or so inches apart, then nodded at the ground. More work! Okay, so this is what I had signed up for, but wouldn't it have been easier to train me up with someone who made some sort of sound? Or was he just trying to live up to his name? We scuffled away at the soil for another half an hour or so. Then he took his headphones off and I decided I would try and catch him out.

'You reckon Messi's gonna sign for Crusaders, Heath? No? You think Ronaldo is *actually* a ladyboy? No, me neither. Hey, Heath, why are babies good at football? Because they're dribblers. Get it? Dribblers?'

Nothing. Absolutely nothing. Just dark hair covering a glum face. And brownish eyes that never looked right at you.

A different tactic: 'Hey, what do you listen to on the headphones? Opera? *Les Mis*? One Direction?'

No response.

Shame. I really wanted to know actually.

'Hiya. You Ben?'

For a minute I thought Heath had thrown his voice and made it come out behind me. But it wasn't Heath. It was a girl in a trackie with a pink stone around her neck who just sort of blew the quietness away.

'So you got Horti to start with? That's the easy bit. Wait till you have to get up in the morning to milk the cows! They don't even use machines! *Five* o'clock in the morning!'

'Seriously? What sort of place is this? A Japanese prison camp?'

'Why, what were you expecting here? A Spa Break?' She laughed. A high laugh. Like a song.

'Don't we ever just sit around and, like, get talked to?'

'Yeah, we do,' she said. 'But the work's the main thing. Builds your sense of discipline. *Apparently*.'

'So how long have you been here?' I asked her, taking in her looks. She was fit.

'A month and a bit. I like it. Most of the time.'

She plonked herself down on the grass and twiddled with the stone thing around her neck.

'So what's your story then?' I asked. 'Joyrider? Drugs baron? Parent-hater?'

She turned on me like a feral cat.

'Hey, don't be so bloody smart!' she snapped, her face full of storms. 'Do I look like a druggie – or a parent-hater?'

'No, no, of course not! It – it was just a joke,' I stuttered.

How was I to know my smooth-talking irony wouldn't work on her?

'Drugs are no joke! Neither's joyriding. And my mum is my best friend in the whole wide world! So, if you go around here making gags like that you won't make many mates.' She scowled, turning her head away.

Okay, so I'd got it wrong. My sense of humour

obviously wasn't going to be appreciated around here. Dad was always telling me that 'sarcasm is the lowest form of wit' but hey, what did he know?

The girl pushed a strand of chocolate-brown hair back and seemed to soften a bit. Then Heath sat down beside her and took her hand in his. She gave him a funny smile and then it seemed as if everything was back to normal. Whatever that was!

Heath got up and went on with his silent digging and she started blathering about the farm.

'Didn't get much fresh air at home,' she said. 'Couldn't leave Mum, you see. But it's gorgeous out here, isn't it? Look! See that? That's barley. You can tell because it's got a sort of beard. They'll cut it in the autumn time. Mind you, we won't be around to see it.'

Strangely enough, I was finding it real hard to get excited about barley, but she was so into it that I nodded my head once or twice to look as if I was interested. Then she started explaining the differences between barley and wheat and if it hadn't been for those blue eyes and cute dimples I swear I'd have lost the will to live.

'See this area?' she said. 'There have been people around these parts for over 9,000 years. Imagine!'

'Yeah, imagine!'

A mist had thickened up around us, hiding the sun. Good old Irish weather.

'Knockmore – *An Cnoc Mór* – it means Big Hill,' she breathed. 'Did you know that?'

I did actually. Part of my Google search before I got myself signed in. Not that I was interested in centuries-old history. That was more my gran's department.

'You wanna go down to the shore tomorrow maybe? Skim a few pebbles?' she asked.

'Okay,' I said reluctantly. I love to *look* at the sea – I'm just not so good when I'm in it. 'Are we allowed?'

'Sure. Fresh sea air – all part of our "healing".'

'Whatever,' I said. 'You know what? I don't even know your name.'

'Lauren,' she answered with another megawatt smile. 'Lauren Murray. All the way from Simon Street.'

Now *this* got my attention. I could see *Simon Street*, written in an adult hand, and then copied in a red crayon scrawl. Suddenly it felt like the air had needles in it.

Chapter three

'Okay, folks, take a seat and let's get started.'

Some small guy with a baseball cap on back-to-front and a beard like Captain Birdseye was organising us into a big circle.

'Who's he?' I asked Lauren.

'That's Chris. He's one of the behaviour specialists. We do this every evening after dinner.' Then she mimicked in some kind of weird American accent: *'Get ready for Circle Time!'*

And she laughed that high laugh again, and I knew I should have sat somewhere else. I didn't need anyone getting under my skin. I had one purpose here and I didn't need any distractions, but it was hard to sit beside some fat bloke when you could have a looker like Lauren beside you. With that smile.

'Ben, you're new to the group,' said Baseball Cap. 'Would you like to introduce yourself?'

'Em, let me think. No!' I answered.

Evidently that was the wrong response.

'*Okaay*. We'll leave it until you're ready then,' he said. 'If that's how you feel?'

It should have been a statement but I could tell by his raised eyebrow it was a question in disguise.

'That's how I feel,' I smiled.

'Great, we'll move on then,' he said.

I swear he was speaking through clenched teeth. I was obviously making a big impression on these guys.

'Lauren? Would you like to tell us about your day?'

Didn't these guys know not to ask closed questions? Jesus, what sort of counsellors were they? Lauren dutifully obliged though.

'Well, I cleaned out the stables and gave Sky a bit of a groom. She loves the body-brush on her skin. Then I met Ben here and got talking and that. And then helped out in the canteen. That was about it!' Her singsong voice tipped upwards at the end, Belfast style.

'Well, thank you for making our newcomer feel welcome, Lauren. Is he settling in?'

Hey! Wait a minute – this was finding out about me by default! That was cheating!

'Think so – but he's no farm boy!' she laughed.

'Is that right?' Beardy Baseball Cap asked with a sneaky smile. 'And what have Ben's duties been today?'

'Hey, you can't do that!' I protested.

'What's that, Ben?'

'Ask her questions about me. You can't get information out of me through her – that's, that's – I don't know what it is, but it's flippin' sly!'

These guys weren't going to make a sucker out of me, coming at me sideways like that.

'Sorry, Ben. I was just interested in Lauren's perspective. If information about you is a no-go area I will respect that.'

'It's not no-go. It's just go-slow. I'll tell you when I'm good and ready.'

He nodded his head with his eyes closed like he was some sort of priest.

Plonker! I knew what he was at, but Lauren was looking at me like I'd been let loose from a cage.

'I just don't like people being sneaky, that's all,' I mumbled to her. Which I suppose was a bit rich coming from me! I'd sneaked my way in here and hadn't told anyone the truth.

She pushed her stray strand of hair back again and rolled her eyes like I was some sort of drama queen. Maybe she was right. I had got myself in here so maybe I should cooperate more. Play along.

Then I saw the song-thrush eyes again and sort of shivered as Allie Cooper stared at me. She was standing in the doorway as if she was waiting for something.

'Allie?' asked Baseball Cap.

'Oh, hi, Chris. Sorry to interrupt. I just wanted to give out the duty rota for tomorrow. Is it okay if I do it now?'

'Sure, go ahead.'

'Frank, Conor, Shane and Heath, you're mucking out the stables. Lauren, Erin, Philip and Ben, you'll check on the cattle, move them into the next field and fill up their water trough. The rest of you are on chicken duty.'

'What about the afternoon?' called out a squeaky voice. Some little turd with a mop of curly brown hair was actually asking for *more* work!

'The afternoon's free, Zach,' said Allie. 'Temperatures are going to be in the top twenties, so John has decided you can all have time off to enjoy the sun.'

'See? I told you we'd get to go down to the shore,' whispered Lauren. 'I have my sources, you know.' She tapped the side of her nose as she said this, then winked over at Allie.

And one song-thrush eye winked back.

Chapter four

'The water washes the sand away from under your feet,' Lauren was saying, between fits of giggles. 'It's like a big hole waiting to swallow you up.'

'Jesus, have you never seen sand before?' scoffed Frank Morgan.

He was sitting brooding on the bank, giving everybody dirty looks under his mop of red hair. Including Lauren.

'Yeah, I've seen sand before, Frank! But who was talkin' to you anyway?'

No flies on this girl – she clearly gave as good as she got.

I watched Frank glare back at her and wondered what his problem was. Then I saw Heath watching *him*. Well, sort of glaring strangely through strands of brown fringe.

Lauren and a few of the other girls ran further into the water.

'Bloody hell, it's freezing!' squealed Lauren, laughing her head off.

What was she expecting? The Mediterranean?

The lough in front of us was littered with pladdies (little islands to you, if you don't know the word) and craggy-looking rocks. And, in case you don't know, Strangford Lough isn't really a lake – it's a great big inlet of the sea.

It obviously didn't take Lauren long to warm up. She started splashing Erin and another girl and the next thing I knew she was throwing water all over me too.

'Hey! Thanks for the shower!' I shouted.

'No point coming down to the sea and staying dry,' she laughed.

So I waded in and joined in the splash-fest, jeans rolled up to my knees. Don't know why I bothered – they were soaked anyway. I looked down at my skinny, white legs: not a good look. Lauren's skin was sort of olive-coloured. It suited her. Suited the long dark hair that she was throwing back in an arc, like something out of a shampoo advert.

'Come on, Ben, you can do better than that!' she

laughed and soaked me again.

I tried running after her but running in water is no mean feat, so, being the cool dude that I am, I ended up face down in foam. For a split second I thought I'd stopped breathing. I hated, *hated* being face down in water! Dad had had this bright idea of throwing me into a swimming pool when I was four and ever since that I have had *the* most intense fear of water. When I pulled my head out of the lough, the salt was burning my eyes and nose and blistering at the back of my throat. I shook my head like a dog and caught my breath.

'*Hey, frig off, Parker!*' Frank Morgan shouted.

'Frig off yourself!' I answered.

'You soaked me, you cretin!'

'Who are you calling a cretin?' I asked. Very manfully.

'You, you dork! You got hearin' problems as well as crap eyesight?'

'What are you on about?'

'Well, you must be blind to friggin' fancy Lauren Murray! Look at her – all skin and friggin' bones!'

And then he spat. A big slobbery, foaming spit.

Did I fancy Lauren? I was busy working this out instead of cuffing Frank Morgan when I saw Heath walking towards him. And it all seemed to happen so quickly. One minute Frankie Boy was hunched up scowling on the grass and the next he was being dragged into the water by the neck of his shirt. He was kicking like a bloody foal and raging obscenities all around him, but Heath just wordlessly pulled him into the water. Then he held his head down. And kept holding his head down.

Okay, so Frank Morgan was obviously a prat, but by this stage he needed to get up for air. And still Heath held him down. Shit! I had to do something.

'Heath? Heath? Let him *go*!'

I tried pulling Heath off him but nothing. No let up. No words.

'Jesus, Heath – you're going to friggin' drown him!' I tried to wrench him off Frank Morgan but this guy was as strong as a pit bull in heat.

'Heath? It's okay. Let him go now. Please, Heath.'

It was Lauren now, almost whispering to him, holding his arm like he was fragile or something. But still he held Frank under the water.

'Heath, *please* – let him go,' she said again.

And then he did let go. He turned and walked slowly back out of the water, heaved himself up the bank and strolled out of sight as if he hadn't just attempted to murder someone. Holy crap! The sea breathed again, in and out, and I just stood there and watched: watched Lauren watching Heath, watched Frank Morgan spluttering and gasping for breath and watched the rest of the gang getting back to doing whatever they were doing before. This was obviously normal behaviour around here.

'It's okay, he'll be fine,' Lauren said, but she was talking about Heath, not Frank.

'*He – he could have killed him!*' I said in a voice that came out so high-pitched I looked around to check it hadn't come from someone else.

'Heath was just protecting me. That's what he does,' she said with a shrug, like drowning someone was no big deal.

Frank was sloping off the beach and throwing himself on the bank like he'd swum the Atlantic. Nobody, *nobody* checked to see if he was okay.

'This is crazy! We need to tell somebody about this! Frank might need medical attention or something. And Heath, well, Heath might need ...'

'What?' she asked.

'I don't know. To be tranquillised or something. He can't just go around trying to kill people!' I squawked.

'Stop panicking! We'll tell them later. Heath just needs some time out and Frank's okay – he's breathing, isn't he? Don't make such a drama out of it.'

She was drying her hair with a towel as if it was just a normal summer afternoon: a few kids splashing at the seaside, having fun, trying to exterminate one another. Frank's gangly white body lying on the bank, gasping for breath. Perfectly normal summertime behaviour at Knockmore Farm. What kind of freakin' place *was* this?

Chapter five

Heath didn't come to Circle Time that evening. I thought maybe he'd been expelled or something, though I wasn't sure if you could actually get expelled from Knockmore. Frank sat in the circle with a face on him that could have turned milk sour.

'So what's Frank got against you?' I whispered to Lauren.

'Nothing. He just fancies me, that's all.'

'And that's how he shows it? By throwing insults around? Boy! The lad's got class!' I shook my head.

'That's how a lot of boys are, the ones I know anyway. You don't show your feelings in Simon Street – you do the opposite,' she shrugged.

I straightened up. 'Is *he* from Simon Street too?'

'Yep. So's Allie, the farm manager. That's why she kinda keeps an eye on us. She lived next door to ours before I was born.'

'Ri-ight,' I said. Slowly. Turning thoughts around in my head. 'And Heath? Where does he come from?'

'Who knows? He doesn't speak – remember?'

'But I'm guessing he fancies you too, right? Hence the attempted murder scene?'

'He wasn't going to murder him, you plonker!' she scoffed at me. 'He was just teaching Frank a lesson. He needs one every once in a while.'

So Knockmore operated on some kind of jungle justice then. Good to know.

Lauren was fiddling with the pink stone around her neck again, and smiling at Allie Cooper who was coming through the door.

'Hi, guys.'

'Hi, Allie,' was the mumbled reply from the group.

Allie sat down and addressed us.

'Instead of Circle Time tonight we're going to talk about farm management,' she said, smiling round the room. 'Some of you have been here a few days, some a few weeks, even months. One or two of you are actually ready to leave us soon. And some of you might have heard what I'm about to say several times already – so be patient! I want to talk to you today about how this place works. You need to understand that the physical effort, the daily chores involved on the farm, will hopefully help you to take stock and think. About perspectives, about yourselves, about relationships. I grew up in the inner city. I wouldn't have recognised a bullock if it hit me in the face! But I knew that I loved animals even though I knew so little about them. And I knew that animals – and the countryside – had a kind of healing power. I'm hoping that you find that too or have already found that here.'

She looked at us with such hope in her face I thought it best to nod my head.

'Ben, you seem to understand,' she said with a smile. 'Something happens, doesn't it? It's like you've taken a step back in time to where distractions like Facebook and *Grand Theft Auto* don't exist. The magic of the farm makes you face up to things, doesn't it?'

Her voice was having a weird hypnotic effect on me. She had this sort of choppy fringe that she kept blowing pointlessly out of her eyes. Her eyes speckled with little brown dots.

'Ben?'

'Em, yeah,' I replied. A man of many words.

'Do you want to elaborate?'

Actually, no, I didn't, but I was beginning to learn that questions around here weren't really questions, so I thought I'd better roll with it. I shifted in my seat and tried to think of the right answer. Something profound. Trouble was, all I could think about was the attempted *Midsomer Murder* down on the beach and the welts on my hands from digging soil. She was still smiling at me, probing me with those song-thrush eyes.

'I miss my wee sister,' I said.

Jesus, where did *that* come from?

'Okay, Ben. Do you want to tell us about Amy?'

How did she know Amy's name?

'Well, she's seven, going on twenty-seven. She's crazy about snakes. And tarantulas. And all things disgusting.'

'Yes,' she coughed, 'we know about the snakes.' Her eyes sort of flicked in embarrassment. 'And how does Amy feel about you being here?'

'Not great. Sad, I suppose.'

Okay, so she was making me feel guilty now. Trying to get me to think about how my actions affected other people. Clever.

'But, she'll understand some day,' I said. 'When I explain everything to her.'

Allie's forehead wrinkled up into creases. I'd confused her now. And I decided I'd said enough –

it was time she moved on to someone else. I put my head in my hands and waited for her to take the hint. She moved on to Erin Freeman and asked her about the chickens.

Lauren nudged me in a kind of nice way and all of a sudden I felt exhausted. Exhausted from farm work, exhausted from talking about myself, exhausted from near-death on the lough and exhausted from keeping secrets. And then out of the blue I wanted to go home. I even wanted to speak to Mum and Dad. *Without* having an argument. I was fourteen and all of a sudden I felt like a friggin' baby. Maybe this whole thing was one ginormous mistake!

But Allie's voice was still rising and falling.

'So, let's talk a little about the structure of Knockmore,' she was saying now. 'How it works, that sort of thing. Most of you already know but, for those of you who are new, let me explain. Each of you will follow a structured daily programme that will help you to develop positive behaviours. We want you to be more mindful, I suppose, of how others act and feel – including animals. With guidance from us we're hoping that you'll make new connections with friends, with family, with nature.'

I had no idea what my personal programme was

going to be, but there was no bloody way I was making any connections with that crazy brown bull in the top field. No way! Allie Cooper could nod her head at me until the rest of the freakin' cows came home!

'And, to sum up, that's what we do here, kids – self-reflection, simple living, engaging work – we hope through these that you will learn to like yourselves again.'

I kind of thought she was looking hopefully at me again, checking out whether or not I was up for the deal. I nodded back. Picked my fingernails and hoped I'd find what I needed here.

Chapter six

A noise like a bloody siren went off, knocking me
out of my tropical pool with prerequisite waterfall
and gorgeous shampoo girl. Well, Lauren Murray
actually.

'What the hell is that?'

'That, Ben, is your early-morning wake-up call,'
announced Jack the Lad with his usual smirk and
bulging biceps, as he turned off the shrieking alarm
on the mobile phone he'd been holding against my
ear. 'I believe you're on milking duty?'

'And I believe you're supposed to knock before
you enter?' I countered – equally smirkily.

'There are no locked doors and no secrets in
Knockmore, matey!'

You want to bet? *Matey*!

My eyes felt like they were filled with glue as I stumbled down the stairs after him. I hadn't even had breakfast!

'I've put you with Heath again. He really seemed to gel with you the other day when you worked together in Horti.'

He did? So silence and glares equalled gelling in this place? Well, I suppose he hadn't tried to drown me, so maybe with Heath that counted as friendship.

'Clean your hands before milking, as well as the cow's teat and the bucket you're going to be collecting the milk in. If you're not careful about hygiene it'll affect the quality of the milk – and we're going to be drinking this stuff.'

And off he went. Again. Marching across the walkway and just leaving me to it. And to Silent Boy.

'Right, Heath,' I said. 'I know you don't talk and stuff, but you're really going to have to help me out here. The closest I've been to a teat was my wee sister's milk bottle, like six years ago, and that didn't have a great big, fat, heaving heifer attached to it. With back legs that might kick me the minute I go near those udder things. Jesus, look at the size of them!'

I stood for a minute. Speechless. All I could think of was Katie Price/aka Jordan in the Australian jungle.

Heath sat me down on a stool beside Jordan, then wordlessly fetched a bucket and put it between my knees. He took a strip of cloth and tied the cow's back legs together, then made a squeezing motion with his hands and left me to it. Then he sat down beside Jordan's mate, pulled on his headphones, and started squishing away like he'd been born to it.

No way was I going to drink that stuff! No way, *José*! My milk came nicely out of a green-and-white carton, thank you, not out of a freakin' *cow*! The place smelt like – well, sour milk.

'Hiya!'

The high voice again. The shampoo hair.

'I swapped so I'm on with you two.'

How was she so bloody chirpy at ten minutes past five in the morning?

'You *swapped*? To get up in the middle of the night and squeeze a cow's udders?'

'Yeah, I love this time of the morning. I don't know – it's just so fresh or something. Mum was never awake until afternoon so morning was always *my* time.'

Lauren had mentioned her mum a few times, like she was some sort of invalid or something.

'Do you, like – look after your mum?' I asked. Hoping she wasn't going to turn on me again like she did with the drugs thing.

'Most of the time, yeah. Sometimes Nana helps. Mainly me though. But, hey, enough talk – these mammas won't milk themselves!'

She patted Heath on the shoulder, sat down to Katie Price III next to me and grabbed two teats. Then kept talking.

'Have you ever been to Africa, Ben?'

'Em, no. Should I?'

'I'd love to go to Africa!' she sighed. 'Lions, tigers, elephants, pandas!'

Pandas? In Africa?

She smiled over at Heath and proceeded to pull and squirt almost in rhythm with her Silent but Deadly Friend. There was obviously a knack to this milking lark and I wasn't getting it.

'When I win the EuroMillions I'm defo going to Africa! I'll pay for you and Heath to come too, okay? But you'll have to start developing an *empathy* with animals first, Ben.'

Being empathetic with animals could land you in jail in some places, but I desisted from pointing this out. Anyway, I didn't want to break Lauren's daydream. She looked all pensive and sort of enchanted, sitting there flicking her hair and thinking about the African savannahs. Or was she in China? She talked away to the cow as she milked it, coaxing it, cajoling it – apparently its real name was Daisy – and had half a bucket of milk before I had more than a dribble.

I stopped trying.

She glanced into my bucket and grimaced. 'Look, catch the teat up high like this, with your thumb and first finger – then squeeze down with the other fingers.' She ran her other three fingers down the teat and the milk spurted out. 'And repeat!'

I gave it a go. And it worked. A weak spurt but a spurt nevertheless.

'You got it!' She grinned at me. 'Two teats at a time – one, two, one, two – and you'll swing into the rhythm.'

So I struggled on, with some success. But little rhythm.

'Wouldn't you take your mum?' I asked after a while. 'To Africa?'

'Defo. It would only be for a few weeks,' she said, getting all excited. 'Maybe a month. We could go on one of those jeep safaris and see everything close up.'

I must admit, I was beginning to like the sound of it.

'So you do the Euro lotto thing then?' I asked.

'Don't be daft – I'm not even eighteen! Nana does it for me. In the bookies' at the end of our street. She usually does a few horses for me too, but I never win on those. Never really read up on their form, just pick a name I like and hope for the best.'

I couldn't imagine my gran going anywhere *near* a bookies'! In fact, she probably didn't even know what a bookies' *was*. Clearly, I'd led a sheltered life, but then, I already knew that. My next life, on the other hand – well, that was a mystery waiting to unfold.

'So do you reckon your mum would let you go?' she asked. 'She looked sort of *careful* – don't think Africa would be up her street, would it?'

'When did you see my mum?' I asked. Guarded.

'When she dropped you off, bozo! Your mum, your dad and your wee sister. All very middle class,' she added in a stupid crusty sort of voice.

'We are what we are,' I huffed. 'Can't help it if they've got good jobs.'

'Of course you can't! You can't help it if you're privileged, Ben. And well off and suburban and safe.'

She was hard as a pebble now, firm as wire. Her hair was crunched into a ponytail at the nape of her neck, as if it had a temper. Needed to be held back. When did the wind change?

'Why *are* you here anyway, Ben? What did you do in your safe world that made your safe parents send you to this safe place?' she asked, staring at me.

Even Heath was watching. In fact, the bloody cow was watching, probably relieved that I had stopped torturing its teats.

'Same as you,' I answered. 'Time out. Time to get a hold of things.'

'Bollocks!' she said.

And flicked her hair away like a scorpion's tail. Obviously I was fooling no-one. Maybe it was time to 'fess up to these guys about why I was really here.

Chapter seven

Of course, three cows didn't provide enough milk for the entire centre. The rest was bought in – sly or what? But Katie Price and her mates were supposed to make us feel *useful*. Right. Who thought up this crap? After milking duty, I discovered I was also on breakfast duty, dishing out plates of cereal and toast for the troubled teens of Norn Iron – that's Northern Ireland to you. Apart from Frank and Heath, I couldn't see much wrong with any of them. I reckoned this was just some sort of respite centre for lazy, middle-class parents.

'Hello there, Ben. Getting on alright?'

John Wilson, aka the Honcho, suddenly spoke from behind me.

'Er, yeah. Thanks.'

'Have you taken the time to venture around Knockmore yet? Properly, I mean? We have acres of interesting farmland here, rich in historical heritage. You know there's a monastic settlement nearby? At Nendrum? A bright young man like you would find that very interesting, I should think.'

Would I? Monks running around in black cloaks?

'It dates back to the fifth century. Fascinating, isn't it?'

There was the stupid smile again. And the comb-over blowing in the breeze. I didn't know whether he was just striking up conversation or *telling* me to go to the settlement. You never knew around here what people were actually trying to say to you. Especially when their hair kept switching sides on their head. The Honcho handed me a map before I'd even made my mind up. Okay then, I'd go to the bloody monastery that afternoon – pass a bit of time anyway.

'I think you'll find what you're looking for there,' he said. And winked. Actually *winked*!

And how did he know what I was looking for? Or that I was looking for *anything*? Like I said before, this Honcho was one weird dude. There was something – something just not quite right about him.

There were just over twenty acres of land around

Knockmore. Wooded bits, flat bits, hilly bits, wet bits. A bozo like me could get lost around here. Traipsing around the countryside was never really my thing, but it was actually good to get away from the rest for a bit. And I liked the fact that no matter where you went you could smell the lough. It was low tide at the minute and the mud was dark-coloured and sort of firm-looking. I could see birds stalking over it, sifting for prey probably.

I stared at the wide, low sky and thought of Amy. I should have hated my wee sister really, but I didn't. I couldn't. She was the natural child and I was the cuckoo in the nest, but it didn't change the fact that I loved her to bits. It bloody well changed how I felt about *them* though. Why they waited till my fourteenth birthday to drop a bombshell like that I'd never know! Letting me go around for twelve years thinking I was the son and heir when I was just some bloody abandoned toddler they took in because they couldn't have their own! Even *that* bit was a lie, cos they had Amy five years later, all by themselves – no fostering, no adoptions, no IV Bloody F!

I walked along the coastal path for a bit and brooded. Like Heathcliff. Until I found the bones of a ruined cottage near the shore and went in and just sat. There was a smell like piss mixed with seaweed.

There was no roof left and just two rooms and a door to the front facing the sea. Probably a fisherman's cottage or something. Jesus, people lived, like, really modestly in the past. Our house at home was at least five times the size of this. I couldn't imagine me, Mum, Dad and Amy cooped up in two rooms – we'd kill each other. Well, we wouldn't really, cos Mum would make us talk through our *issues* and Dad would just disappear off to his computer until the storm was over. Mum acted like a social worker 24/7 and Dad acted like a – whatever he was with computers – 24/friggin'/11!

I looked out through a window the size of a calendar and wondered what Freddy Fisherman and his wife got up to in the old days. They probably had tons of kiddies running around this old cottage – or did they spend all their time playing on the beach? Or helping their dad haul nets in full of wriggling fish to feed the five thousand? Mrs Fisherman probably spent all day cooking and cleaning and wiping asses and Freddy probably drowned his sorrows in the evenings with a pot of poteen. Or something. Ah, those were the days! No controlled assessments, no modular exams, no 'Ben, you need to think what you're going to do with your life'. You would have just got up, eaten your gruel, worked a sixteen-hour day, drunk whiskey and gone to bed. If you were an adult, that is. But now you had to 'think about your choices' and do stupid exams and find out your parents are just a couple of liars. Was I feeling sorry for myself? Bloody right I was!

'Hey! Bugger off! This is my place!'

The dulcet tones of the one and only Frank Morgan. So much for getting away from them all.

'What, you own this cottage? Like you paid for it in cash or something?' I yelled back.

'No, dickhead. But I still own it. Clear off and find your own hideout!'

Hideout? Did Frankie think he was in an Enid Blyton novel?

'I'm going nowhere, Frankie. The Honcho sent me off to 'find myself' today, and that's exactly what I'm doing.'

'Call me Frankie again and I'll give you a face like the back-end of a Boxer dog!' he bawled.

Interesting use of simile. I wondered if the back-end of a Boxer looked much different from the back-end of any other dog?

'What is your problem, Frankie? Were you, like, born in a bad mood?'

I didn't quite get the answer to that because he had swung towards me and knocked me over with a yowl like a friggin' Howler Monkey. I fell out

53

through the door and we rolled around like two cavemen on the grass bank beside this forgotten cottage, and I swear it was better therapy than all the Circle Time put together!

'Don't you friggin' tell me I'm in a bad mood! I'll show you a friggin' bad mood!' he shouted.

Frankie was a lad of rich vocabulary.

'Okay, okay, so you were in a good mood! Only it was hard to tell!' I screamed back, flipping him over and landing him strategically on a sharp piece of rock sticking upwards.

'Aaaaaaaaaahhhh! That friggin' hurt, man! You plonker!'

He was really howling now, holding his bits like they might fall off at any minute.

'I'll probably never have children now, thanks to you, you ...'

He was in that much pain he couldn't think of a suitable insult. I was just relieved that I might have put an end to the possibility of more wee Frankies running about. He got up and did some kind of dance now, a one-footed version with hands placed tightly between legs.

'What the bloody hell did you have to come here for?' he yelled. *'Bad enough I've seen that prat Wilson snooping around here!'*

'It's just an old cottage. On a farm, Frankie. What the hell is the big deal?'

He would have swung at me again but that would have meant letting go of his precious gems, so I reckoned I was safe enough.

'It's old Miller's place,' he said. 'The oul' fella that used to live next door to me – he used to bring me here. We used to gut fish here and take them home to my da.'

That was a total of four sentences from Frankie – more than I'd ever heard him put together without a curse word. Jesus, he was going all nostalgic or something on me! He ran a hand through his mop of red hair and I swear I thought he was going to cry on me.

'So you've been around here before?' I asked him.

'Yeah, used to come here all the time. That's why I wanted to come back.'

Come back? Another bozo had got himself signed in? I wasn't the only one?

'So how'd you manage it? Get back, I mean?' I was curious now.

'Just stole a few cars. Nothing big,' he shrugged.

I wondered what he considered big. But I decided not to ask.

'How'd'you know they'd send you *here*?'

'Asked the social worker if she knew the place. She showed me a picture on the net and then agreed to sort it for me.'

He had released one hand from his bits by this stage but his face was still twisted up like a – like a – *front* end of a Boxer dog.

'Sorry about that, mate,' I said, nodding at his crown jewels.

''S'alright,' he mumbled. 'They're made of stern stuff. But don't call me friggin' Frankie again, right?'

'Okay, I won't call you Friggin' Frankie. So this oul' fella – is he still alive?'

'Nah. If he was, I'd be alright, wouldn't I? But he kicked the bucket last year,' he said stiffly, his jaw hard.

'What was his name?'

'Joe. And if you tell anybody any of this – Ben*nie* – I'll come after you and knock seven bells out of you!'

'Got it.'

'Now frig off out of my place and go and do your bloody soul-searchin' somewhere else!' he said, still clutching.

Clearly our bonding session was over. I wouldn't normally have taken orders from Frankie, but the lad needed time out and I knew what that was like. Plus, I had a monastery to visit.

I walked on, imagining the wee town of Strangford in the distance. I remembered going there with Mum and Dad before Amy was born –

taking the ferry across to Portaferry and visiting the aquarium. Just the three of us. There wasn't a computer in sight so I had Dad's full attention all day. Actually, he got a *bit* overexcited that day about divers feeding sharks or congers or something in the open sea tank. It was like *so* embarrassing! I liked the seals the best though. The pups in the nursery pond – they were sort of cool. Nearly ready for their next leap into the wild. A bit like us sad lot at the farm.

After a week's incarceration I would have my first family visit and I just knew I'd get ninety questions from Mum about rediscovering myself. I wouldn't friggin' have to rediscover myself if I knew who I was in the first place. Ben Parker? Or some sap called Eddie Rogan? Couldn't they have broken it to me gently? Not: *'Happy Birthday to you, and by the way you're adopted!'* Not: *'Here's your present, Ben, oh and a whole new identity.'* A new iPod and ID in one day. So much for Mum's super social-worker skills – she just came right out with it and expected me to dust myself off and get on with being a whole new person. And Dad expected me to be grateful! Bollocks to them – I'd tell the Honcho that I didn't want the visit. It was up to me after all. Amy would probably be disappointed but they'd buy her a rat or something to cheer her up. As long as she was surrounded by rodents and reptiles she was happy enough.

When I dragged myself to the top of the hill I saw the remains of the monastery. And I was blown away! I know, crazy or what – getting excited about three dry-stone walls and a stump of a round tower, but it was the fact that it just stood there, all alone, after more than fifteen hundred years! Those big stones must have been dragged up there by men with muscles the size of the Mountains of Mourne! Awesome. And some guy called Mochaoi lived there (apparently you say it like 'Maughee') and called all the other monks to prayer. Turned out he was St Patrick's buddy. I was beginning to think Knockmore and the surrounding area were actually a *bit* interesting. Maybe not as interesting as, say, *Abyss* or *SMT Devil Survivor*, but interesting. In a history sort of way. Maybe I might even learn a thing or two while I was here. Maybe.

Chapter eight

'Seriously – fifteen hundred years!'

I was still going on about the monastery at dinner that evening. Lauren was looking at me with a sort of weird smile, like she was laughing at me. She exhaled a little. Like a kettle.

'Jesus, Ben! You're actually getting *interested* in something around here. What happened? Did someone give you happy pills?'

'No, but the Honcho made me go. Oh, and I ran into Frank Morgan on the way,' I said. 'Boy, does he have *issues*!'

'Frank's not had it easy. He'll work it all out eventually though.'

There she was, twiddling with the pink stone

again and being all *empathetic*. She seemed to get everybody around here. Including me. I leaned towards her and mentioned what he'd told me about getting himself put in here.

'Yeah, I know,' she said, more seriously now. 'So did I.'

'You as well?' I asked in my stupid shrieky voice that I reserved for moments of surprise. 'What sort of place is this that everybody goes around getting themselves *in*?'

'Everybody?' she asked, raising one eyebrow at me.

'Well, I mean – you, and Frank. Not everybody. Obviously. But seriously, what's the story with this place?'

'You sound like an undercover reporter or something,' she laughed. 'Ben Parker – Undercover Investigator. Jesus, you'll be getting yourself one of those silly hats. And a mac – like Columbo!'

Who?

Lauren had done it again – gone from being all serious to just messing about in five seconds flat. Any time you thought she was going to pour her heart out or something, she'd just laugh everything off. I watched her cut her fish up into like a thousand pieces, and try to eat her dinner as if we hadn't just had this conversation. She waved Heath over to join us which I was *not* happy about. How was I going to get any more goss with him around, being all menacing and broody and stuff?

'Hi, Heath,' Lauren said. 'Busy day? What's that you've got – the pasta? I didn't fancy the carbonara sauce.'

She chattered away to him as if it was a two-way conversation. But he didn't seem to mind. Just ate his pasta and didn't say a word. Maybe silence was like noise for him: a huge, dark silence pressed against his ears. Right now he only had eyes for his dinner – and the rest of us, well, we might as well have not been around.

I was sort of wishing I could say the same for Zach. That guy told *the* worst jokes ever. Every mealtime he'd rock up with yet another crap one – 'What's a pirate's favourite letter? *Arrgh!* Get it?' No, Zach, now bog off, I wanted to say, but everybody else seemed to practically wet themselves laughing.

Lauren was right about the investigator bit, though. I *had* come here to uncover something, but I was getting more and more distracted by my fellow *inmates*. Their stories were starting to become more interesting than my own. Me and my middle-class upbringing – yeah, Lauren had been right about that too. Ben Parker and his rebellion without a cause. That's what my teachers thought, that's what Gran thought, and most likely that's even what Amy thought. I was just one big teenage chip-on-my-shoulder nerd. At least that's what I think Lauren saw when she looked at me with that lopsided grin.

'Right, everybody! Circle Time in fifteen minutes!'

Chris was coming round the tables, practically rubbing his hands in glee at the prospect of more of our dysfunctional stories. I wasn't even close to finishing my dinner – Jesus, they didn't even give you time to take a leak around here!

'Nendrum Room – right at the end of the corridor!' he called out.

'You coming, Heath?' Lauren was asking.

For reasons probably only known to our Heathcliff, he was allowed to opt out of a lot of meetings and stuff. Stuff the rest of us had to go to. Tonight, though, he was obviously going to honour us with his company, because he followed Lauren down the corridor and took a seat right beside her. Was I missing something?

I sat on the other side of her and wondered what he had that I didn't. Apart from being tall, dark and handsome. And apart from a face like Johnny Depp. What could she possibly *see* in him?

'Okay, guys, thanks to all of you for being so punctual.'

Chris said the word *punctual* like he was in pain or something. Maybe he'd sat on something nasty. Like a rusty nail, maybe. Or a piece of discarded monastery.

'We've been quite lucky with the weather lately which of course is unusual for this Emerald Isle.' He laughed. Unnecessarily. 'So you've all been out and about and making the most of all that Knockmore has to offer. Fresh air, time to reflect, hard work – all these things are character-building and I hope that you have benefited from them. Now, would anybody like to share their experiences from today?'

I was looking around to see which plonker was going to start us off when I noticed Frankie Boy glaring at me. No, not glaring at me, burning friggin' holes in me! I frowned at him in an effort to convey 'What the …?' but then he started grimacing. Like his face was in one of those distorted mirrors.

'What?' I mouthed.

He bunched his two hands up into fists like he was squeezing sponges dry.

'Eh?' I mouthed again.

'Ben, you wish to say something?' asked Chris.

'Er, no.'

'Thought not. You haven't been very forthcoming with us, Ben, have you?'

'Er, no.'

'A man of few words.' He nodded, his floppy baseball cap almost obscuring his eyes. 'You like to speak through your actions, don't you, Ben?' He was using what he obviously thought was a very sage, very wise voice.

'Er, *no!*' What was he on about?

'I noticed you today, fighting. Down at the old cottage. It's not the kind of behaviour we advocate at Knockmore, Ben – choosing a solitary location and laying into one of your peers. What was it all about?'

'Laying into one of my peers? He laid into *me!*' I yelped.

'Typical denial, Ben. You haven't really progressed in the last few days, have you?'

'*Whaaa?* I haven't done a bloody thing wrong!'

'Apart from fighting with Frank? Teasing Heathcliff? Behaving inappropriately with one of your female peers?'

'*What are you on about?*' I squeaked. Behaving inappropriately with a female? No such bloody luck!

'Perhaps it's time you left the room and cooled down a little, Ben. Then you can rejoin us when you're not so – animated.'

'I've only just got here! And I've nothing to cool down about – *you* started it!'

My skin felt like it was tightening.

'Ah yes, the reapportioning of blame, Ben. One of your maladies, I'm afraid.'

He was shaking his head like he was the font of all bloody wisdom. I wanted to strangle him with my bare hands! Worse still, my 'peers' were looking at me like I was some sort of psycho. Jesus, all I had done was sit bloody down!

'Jack, would you like to remove Ben, please?' he said to a shadow at the door.

'Jack's not 'removing' me anywhere! I'm not a friggin' mental case, you know. I'm not like *this* lot!' I glared at Jack. 'Frig away off and keep your hands off me!'

Everyone turned to look at me. Everyone. Complete silence.

'You think everyone in the group is a *mental* case, Ben?' Chris asked quietly.

'No, no, I don't. You, you just bloody wound me up, you freak! I didn't mean it. All I wanted to do was just sit here and let the rest spout off!'

My voice was embarrassingly close to tearful. There was a noise like a heartbeat in my ears.

'Ah, spout off, is that it? Yes, I see. And you're superior to all this, aren't you, Ben?'

'No. *No!* You're putting words in my mouth. You've been doing that since I started here – you and your friggin' psychobabble. Just go and pick on somebody else!'

But he wasn't finished with me yet.

'*Pick on* – interesting turn of phrase. I detected a little of the victim mentality about you on your first day, Ben. I think we've learned a lot about your thoughts and feelings tonight.'

'*You know sweet F.A. about me, you creep!*'

I was really roaring now. Out of control. This bloke was trying to wind me up and, boy, was he succeeding! What sort of bloody counsellor was he? I would be writing one big fat letter of complaint about him when I got out, that was for sure! I had bloody tears of frustration in my eyes now. I literally could have decked him! I could feel my fists clenching. The whole room was watching me. Glaring eyes blinking at me from every corner. Chris the Priss had tricked me into this. He had friggin' goaded me like a bullfighter. And Jack the Lad was just waiting to pounce. Like a cat on a rat.

'Perhaps Ben would like to come with me instead? There's no pressure,' came a different voice. A calm voice. The voice of a song thrush.

Chapter nine

'He friggin' started it! With all that "man of few words" crap – he was just trying to rile me! I *know* he was!'

'And you let him?'

'Well – what was I supposed to do? Just take it?'

I was sitting with Allie now, in a room that was all cream walls and quiet.

'He's the bloody paid professional – I'm the kid, remember?'

'So you see responsible behaviour as the prerogative of adults only, Ben?'

'*No! Why do you lot keep twisting what I'm saying?*' Shouting again.

'Then tell me what you're saying. Start at the beginning.'

And she blew her fringe, settling herself back in the chair like she had all the time in the world. Still quiet. Not quiet tight. Quiet easy.

'Look, I shouldn't even be here. I don't have *problems*,' I explained. 'I got myself put in here!'

'Why?'

'Because there was something I needed to find out.'

She frowned at this, but let it go.

'But maybe I made a mistake,' I said. 'Maybe I should just go home.'

'It's not that simple, Ben. You're here for the duration. The only ones who can sign you out are your parents, and I'm afraid they're not going to do that.'

'How do *you* know?'

'Because we speak to them every day. Keep them informed, and they do likewise. They want you to stay here until you've come to terms with who you are.'

Bollocks to them! This whole thing was my idea and I wasn't going to have Mum and Dad dictate to me! *Mum* and *Dad* – don't know why I even kept calling them that! I trusted them. Trusted them like I trusted the bloody sky!

'Tell me about your mum and dad, Ben,' she said. Soft as a whisper.

'Why?'

'Because you're upset with them right now. Maybe talking about them will help?'

'Bloody right I'm upset! Years and years they've been lying to me! What did I do to deserve that? Eh?'

'To deserve what, Ben? A happy family home? Parents who love you? A little sister who idolises you? Grandparents who miss you? Friends who are wondering where you are?'

God, she was good at this.

'Yeah, alright, alright, I get it. I'm being selfish. But it's all a lie because my parents, my grandparents, my mates – well, they all think I'm Ben Parker, don't they? But I'm not – I'm Eddie Bloody Rogan! And who cares about *him*?'

She fell silent for a few moments, turning her head to look out the window, and I thought she had given up on me. Like everyone else. Then she fixed me with her speckled eyes again.

'You're a bright lad, Ben. You don't need me to tell you that a name changes nothing. You're still the person you always were. Only a little more agitated, maybe. Who are you angry with, Ben? Your parents for adopting you? Yourself because you think you no longer fit in?'

Allie Cooper just got straight to the point. She

had a kind of efficiency that had no time for going round in circles.

'I'm angry that they never told me. Until now. I'm angry with whoever bloody well gave me away. Was I a real minger of a baby or something? And why did they wait until I was two years old before they turfed me out?'

'Your birth parents obviously *couldn't* look after you – for whatever reason – and they did the best thing for you: gave you an opportunity for a new life. A better life. But you've worked all that out already, haven't you?'

She looked at me like she could read my mind. There wasn't much sympathy in those song-thrush eyes, but there was something. Understanding, maybe.

'Ben, you have two choices here. You can keep persecuting everybody for just doing their best for you, or you can get your act together. Show us what you're made of. We know you've got a good future ahead of you, if you just get your brain into gear. Entirely up to you.'

I didn't respond.

'Tell me more about Amy,' she said then, changing tack.

'Amy? Amy's well … she's just my wee sis,' I said, wondering why we had changed course. 'She's only seven and I swear she's afraid of nothing. Absolutely nothing! I think Mum and Dad sometimes wish I was more like her.'

'So *you* are afraid of things?'

'Hell, yeah – everything! Water, weirdos, big brown bulls – you name it! But not Amy. She's got – I dunno – confidence. Nothing fazes her. Maybe you get that from being like, real – not a fake like me.'

'Being adopted doesn't make you fake, Ben. It means they chose you. They wanted you. Can't you try to see the positive in that? I do understand that it must feel really weird. And that's why you're here – to have time out – to see what's important. Maybe time away from home will help you to realise what you've got?'

Her head was leaning to one side as she spoke, as if she was trying to peer inside my brain.

'Your mum and dad, they lost two children before they had you, didn't they?'

How the hell did she know about that? Yeah, there were other babies, natural babies. Half-formed and not fit for this world – so Gran said. Too weak to survive. Mum went to bed for ages apparently. Couldn't face the world – until I came along. And then Dad started smiling again. Though I find *that* hard to believe.

'They love you, Ben,' Allie whispered. 'You're

71

their son, their only son, and this is as hard for them as it is for you. Why do you think they couldn't bring themselves to tell you about the adoption sooner? They want you back, Ben. And so does Amy – Amy needs her brother back. More than anything.'

She opened my hands and pressed the words in like secrets. And then walked out of the room, looking almost as upset as I was.

Chapter ten

'That's what he does. Gets all the anger out of your system so that you'll eventually start opening up.'

Lauren was filling me in on Chris the Priss's methods the following morning over breakfast. I still wasn't convinced.

'Like lancing a boil or something,' she explained, pecking at dry toast and flicking her hair away.

'Well, I'd love to see the handbook *that* method's in!' I said. 'I am so going to get him sacked when I'm out of here!'

'Don't be a prat, Ben. He knows what he's doing. Which is obviously more than you do.'

'What do you mean?'

'Saying we're all mental cases? Acting like you're

different from the rest of us? Acting like you *didn't* get yourself signed in?'

How did she know that? Had she heard me talking to Allie?

Or had Allie told her? Her eyes left mine but I could feel her tighten. Like her body was telling me she was on to me, but the conversation was closed for now. She drank her tea and smiled at Heath through the window, where he was watering his plants in silence. Was Lauren some kind of all-seeing, all-knowing witch? Like the ones in Macbeth only *way* better-looking? But then nearly everyone around here seemed to know things. I was starting to panic. Maybe this was a George Orwell book and like everybody could read your thoughts?

'Lauren?'

'Yeah?' she answered, without turning.

'I don't think you're a mental case.'

'Yeah, but you think Heath is. And Frank. And most of the others,' she said, looking at me now with glinting eyes. 'You need to get over yourself, Ben. You're not Mr Perfect and we're not saddos. We all have our reasons for being here. Just don't judge a book by its cover, okay?'

She scraped her chair back and went outside to Heath. Beneath the tough veneer, she was as brittle as glass.

I couldn't figure any of it out. How many of these guys had cheated their way in here like me? And why? And how did everyone seem to know all about me? Mr Mysterious – about as transparent as a bloody Poly Pocket obviously.

I watched Lauren blowing dandelion clocks outside. She had reverted to her happy self. I wondered where she got that happiness from. Did she buy it in a shop on Simon Street? From what I knew about Simon Street that was pretty unlikely. Rows of rundown redbrick houses and burnt-out cars – that was the image I had in my head. But then, like she said, maybe I shouldn't judge a book by its cover.

'Thanks,' said a voice. 'For last night.'

I looked up as Frankie Boy pushed in beside me with a plate of bacon and eggs.

'What did I do last night?'

'You didn't tout on me and the Joe stuff,' he grunted.

'Is that why you were making faces at me at the start? Warning me off? I told you I wouldn't say anything. Not that I would have got the chance with that prat Chris winding me up.'

'That's just his method,' he said.

At least I think that's what he said, mid-chew on fatty, gristly bacon. For a second I thought about

Martha the Sow out the back and nearly vomited.

'Yeah, so I've heard,' I said. 'Sick bloody method if you ask me.'

'Yeah, but it worked, didn't it? You're sort of – I don't know – less annoying today. Less of a friggin' show-off.'

'Cheers!' I said. 'Well, the *method* doesn't seem to have had much effect on *you*!'

'Yeah, it did. I was ten times angrier than this a couple of weeks ago. What you're seeing is my softer side,' he said, still chewing on gristle.

I really was hoping that wasn't Martha in there. I didn't have much time for pigs but the thought of Martha's fat bits going round and round Frankie Boy's mouth like a washing machine was starting to make me feel almost upset.

'Soft? This is you being *soft*?'

'Yeah. I'd never have told you about Joe before the method. Doesn't mean I'm telling anybody else though. So remember what I said,' and he pulled his tomato-ketchup-covered knife across his throat.

Suddenly I was really glad I'd arrived at Knockmore after *hard* Frankie had departed.

'You want some scrambled egg?' he said then. 'I got these eggs fresh straight out of Bertha this morning.'

'Please tell me Bertha's a hen,' I said, rubbing my

forehead and hoping against hope that he wasn't talking about one of the counsellors or, worse still, one of us lot.

'Course she is. Are you as stupid as you look, Ben*nie*? Anyway, you'll soon find out. You and me, bud – we're on chicken-shit duty this morning.'

'Jesus, I can't wait! Frank*ie*.'

So I rolled my eyes and went on my first date with Frankie Boy. They paired you with everyone at some stage at Knockmore. I couldn't figure out which was worse – Hushed Heath or Fierce Frankie. I'd have preferred Luscious Lauren, but I had a feeling that I might have burned that bridge. For now.

'So this is Henrietta. She's a Maran. Lays nice dark-brown eggs, don't you, sweetheart? What? What are *you* looking at, Ben*nie*?'

I was speechless. Frankie Boy was caressing his feathered friend with more affection than I'd thought him capable of.

'Henrietta?' I coughed. 'You call her … Henrietta?'

'Yeah, why? What's wrong with that? It's her name. You laughing at me, Bennie Boy?'

'Erm, just a bit. Is this the softer side you were talking about earlier? Jesus, if Chris the Priss is going to turn me this soft I'm outta here!'

'Look, if you're going to work with the animals you have to get to know them,' he said, all sagely. 'So stop being a prat and listen to me. You want to know about these hens or not?'

'*Okay then,*' I squeaked. I couldn't wait to find out the name of the next one.

'This is Bertha, the one I was telling you about earlier. She's a Silkie cos she's sort of silky, see? And she's got five toes. Did you know most hens only have four?'

I must have entered some sort of parallel universe where the likes of Frank Morgan took seats on University Challenge to talk about bloody chickens! Lessons in poultry from a guy who would punch you before asking your name. Is this what Knockmore did to you?

'Stop looking at me like that and help me clean out this coop,' he grunted. 'And that nesting box over there needs fresh wood shavings. Get a move on!'

I was beginning to think working with Heath was a better idea. Who'd have guessed Frankie Boy could shout out so many bloody orders?

'So you, eh, you like chickens then, Frankie?' I asked.

'Yeah, they're alright. You sort of get to know them. Everybody thinks they're just chickens, but they're not.'

'They're not?' I ventured, almost afraid of his answer.

'Well, they are chickens. *Obviously*. But they're so much more than that. They've got personalities, you know? Like Henrietta there, she's got a great sense of humour.'

Oh boy, I thought. Where was this going? I didn't know whether to laugh or cry now.

'Yeah, she gets me,' he said. 'Runs after me when I sing to her.'

Holy shit! This was too much!

'You *sing* to her?'

'Yeah, sometimes. Just a bit of One Direction now and again. She likes that new Niall Horan song,' he said. 'Hey, what's wrong, Bennie Boy? You got a pain in your belly or something?'

I was doubled over by this stage, holding my stomach like it was going to fall out. I was in pain alright, but not the sort Frankie thought. My sides were splitting and I seriously needed to get away before I roared in hysterics.

'I – I think I just need to go to the bog, Frankie. Okay?'

'Well, hurry up. That wire mesh needs fixing. Don't want more foxes getting in. Don't think I'll ever get over seeing Annie headless.'

'*Whaaat?*'

'Yeah, a fox got her. Took her head right off. The weird thing was she was still walking around … with no head.'

I couldn't help it. The tears were rushing down my cheeks like two waterfalls. I threw myself face down in the grass. I'd never spent ten minutes quite like this in my life. Jesus, Frankie should be on the stage!

'Ach, don't get that upset over it. These things happen in the wild,' he said. 'They're not pretty but they're a fact of life out here.'

Out here? We were only a twenty-minute drive from Belfast for Christ's sake. I was beginning to get my breath back and was just on the point of making sounds like speech when the Honcho arrived over.

'What's going on here, boys?'

'Ah, Ben's a bit put off by my story about Annie. He's not used to the wild, sir.'

'I see. Well, I'm glad you're putting him in the picture, Frank. It takes a while to adjust to farming life.'

He nodded his head in my direction like I'd learned an important lesson.

'Thank you, Frank. Well done. And Ben? I'm glad to see you're developing an empathy with the animals.'

I was off again! More tears, more sides splitting

like karate chops. It was a good job they thought I was crying or Frankie would have been all over me with his fists by now. I would never look at chickens in the same light again. I was heaving breathlessly into the grass by the time Heath arrived over with chicken feed. He looked at me. Briefly. Then walked past.

'Heath's okay with the animals but he's better out on his own planting and growing and stuff,' said Frank. 'No talking involved that way.'

'Has he *ever* spoken?' I asked.

'Yeah, before his accident.'

'Accident?'

'Yeah, hit and run. Saw it on his records.'

'You looked at his records?'

'Yeah! So what? I look at all the records, even yours.'

'But that's – that's … illegal!'

'And your point is? I'm not in Knockmore cos I'm an angel, you know, Bennie Boy. I'm here cos I'm a 'troubled teen', remember? And it's not my fault if Wilson doesn't log off properly. I'm just testing security, that's all.'

He was topping up water, cooing at the chickens and revealing his history of hacking like it was nothing.

'So this accident? What else do you know about it?' I asked.

'Can't tell you – it's illegal, remember?' he sneered.

'Okay, okay, so I'm not whiter than white either. Spill!'

He shrugged his shoulders. 'It'll cost you.'

'What do you mean?'

'You scratch my back, I'll scratch yours.'

'So what do you want?'

'Put in a good word with Lauren for me. Talk me up a bit. If she starts to act nicer to me, then you get more info.'

'But you called her skin and bones!' I said.

'Yeah, that was just flirtin' talk,' he said with a shrug.

This was *not* going to be easy. Lauren thought Frank was straight out of a cave. And, anyway, I wanted Lauren to act nicer to *me* not Frankie Boy. But I agreed to it. Mr Principled, that's me. It wasn't that I needed to know more about Heath. But for some reason I just kind of wanted to. And I needed to know more about the staff so I could get to the bottom of my own secret mission, and Frankie could be just the boy to help. But I have to admit, I felt a prickle of guilt. Not just about Lauren but about spying on other people's lives. After all, I wouldn't be so keen if they were doing it to me.

Chapter eleven

Two days later and Frankie was ready for action.

'Meet me at Old Miller's place later. There's no Circle Time tonight so we can clear off for a bit.'

Frankie was planning to get a look at the Honcho's computer after muck-out duty. He cleared off to get some of that haylage stuff and I headed on over to the stables. It was my first time looking after the horses and I was looking forward to it. Sort of. Mum had asked me a couple of years back if I fancied learning to ride, but I thought I was way too macho for that, so I said no. I wished I hadn't.

'Hi, Ben. This is Sky, the biggest horse on the farm. She's a gentle giant, aren't you, Sky?'

Allie Cooper was smoothing the horse's nose and

whispering into its ear. She always seemed to turn up without making a sound. Just appear out of nowhere like a shaft of light coming through trees.

'We rescued her, poor thing,' she said. 'She was a hunter. After she served her purpose the owners just neglected her. Dunno how anybody could do that.'

'Yeah, well, I know how she feels,' I grumbled.

'Ben,' she said, looking right into my eyes again, '*you* were *never* neglected! Don't compare yourself to a helpless animal that was beaten and broken. You have *got* to stop that self-pity. It's bringing you down.'

Self-pity was sort of my default setting though, so it was hard to shake it off. But there was something about Allie that made me want to impress her. I didn't want her thinking of me as a spoilt brat.

'How long's she been here then?' I asked, changing the subject.

'About a year or so. Took a while for her to trust us. She was wary, you know? Cynical, I suppose.'

This horse was starting to sound a *lot* like me.

'So what do I do with her?' I asked.

'Feed her. The oats and instructions are over there. Then clear out her stable. I'll take her out for a ride later.'

She motioned me over to Sky, showed me how to hold my hand flat if I was feeding her, told me to where to stroke her.

'Don't ever stand too close behind her though, behind any horse. It spooks them and they might kick out.'

'So how did you learn all this?' I asked her.

'Here. On the farm,' she said as if it was the most natural thing in the world. 'I've learned everything here, Ben.' She turned, look straight at me. 'I hope you will too.'

She really believed all this, believed in Knockmore like it was a cure. I couldn't think of a single sarcastic thing to say. I didn't want to anyway. I wondered what she was like when she wasn't here. All long patterned skirts and wooden bracelets that clinked probably. Maybe a home full of crystals and glass jars.

'*Come on, Ben! Muck-out time!*' shouted Frank. Always one to change the mood.

It turned out he wasn't as keen on horses as he was on chickens. He looked frightened of them even. I turned out to be a bit of a natural. I liked their curiosity, their grainy tongues when they licked me. I could see my reflection in conker-coloured eyes. Maybe the *empathy* thing was finally happening to me?

'I wouldn't go near that Sky if I was you,' said Frank. 'Bit of a nutter if you ask me.'

Dad's saying about pot, kettle and black came into my head.

'Allie says she's just had a bad time. She probably just needs a bit of patience, that's all,' I answered.

'Well, you can be as patient as you like with her, mate. I'm staying clear. Anyway, when I finish off here I'm going to ask Wilson for a meeting.'

'Why?' I asked.

'To get into his office, you bozo.'

'Right, Frank, but he'll be there *in* the office with you. Not exactly conducive to fact-finding on his desktop, is it?'

'*Duuuh!* He's going to get called out, isn't he? Hopefully he'll be in such a hurry he'll forget to lock the door behind him. Then I'll get a wee poke around.'

'Who's going to call him out?'

'*You*, you dork! Tell him there's a fight or something and you can't find any of the counsellors. Tell him anything. Tell him you're having nightmares about headless chickens if you want, but keep him out for as long as you can.'

I didn't like the sound of this. Yes, I needed information about the staff here. Yes, I had sneaked myself in here for just that reason, but hacking into someone's computer? And letting Frank take responsibility for this operation? Sky wasn't the nutter around here – I was.

Just then the mare nuzzled into me and I felt a big

jolt of pride. She was suspicious of people, but she was sort of telling *me* that she liked me. Maybe I wasn't so vile after all.

'Come on, girl – let's get you something to eat.'

And she followed me across the barn, like a foal following its mother. Like I used to follow mine.

Later the rain seemed to come out of nowhere. Days, weeks of sunshine disappeared just like that. It gushed down windows, filled up drains, made ponds in the fields. It was like Armageddon.

Frank had already gone back to his room to prepare for Operation Research. So I said goodbye to Sky and ran like a lunatic across the farm and into the old part of the building, drenched, like a rat drowning.

And bang into the Honcho himself.

'Where did that deluge come from?' he said, without seeming to be actually addressing me.

A week ago I'd have said 'The sky', but I was learning to filter my sarcasm a bit more these days. Save it up for when I needed it.

'One season in this bloody country all year round – the rainy season!' the Honcho was saying to no-one in particular.

I wasn't about to turn into a middle-aged melt by engaging in a conversation about the weather, but I was tempted to point out that we'd so far had an unusually good summer.

He glanced at his watch. 'Must go. Frank Morgan wants to see me.' And, shaking his head, off he went.

I wasn't sure whether the headshaking was about the rain or having a chat with Frankie.

In fact, I wasn't sure of anything. You might say there were a few flaws in our plan. Frankie and I hadn't synchronised our watches, not having any. Was he already in the Honcho's office? How much time did I have? And I needed time because I still hadn't thought up a plausible diversion. I had expected it to come to me in a flash of genius but it hadn't.

I rushed across to Block C to change out of my squelchy shoes before raising some kind of alarm – we each kept clean trainers and socks lined up inside the door.

The TV was on in the relaxation room so I glanced in. Lauren was watching some cop show on the telly. She was twisting the pink stone again, mesmerised by some old guy smoking a cigar. Columbo.

'Hiya!' I called out.

She didn't seem to hear me.

'I met Sky today,' I said.

A flicker of a smile.

'You okay?' I asked.

'Yeah. Why shouldn't I be?'

'You just seem … quiet.'

A shrug of her shoulders was all I got in reply.

'Well, have to go. Got a bit of business with Frankie.'

Her forehead creased a bit at this. Then she just curled her feet underneath her and looked back at the screen, her lips as tight as a clam. Conversation over. She was having an off-day. We all had them, but I hadn't seen Lauren closing in on herself like this before. She was hurting about something but I didn't know what. Her attention was back to the shabby-coated Columbo and I knew I needed to just leave her alone.

Back in the house, I heard Frank yowl at the top of his voice and a scuffle of staff ran past. Apparently there was a savage dog on the loose and he was yelling for the Honcho to come and sort it out.

Frankie was creating his own diversion.

Good old Frankie – who else would think up a mad dog as a way to raid the Honcho's computer?

Chapter twelve

'How did you guess his password?' I asked, leaning back against the stone wall of the cottage.

'What's the most common password in the world, Bennie Boy? The one that you'd never think a place like this would use?'

'I dunno, Frank. You're the expert hacker round here. Farm? Cows? Big udders?'

'"*Password*", you prat! Wilson, the lazy toad, couldn't even be bothered to change it to something else.'

It had taken me some time and a bunch of lies to placate Frankie after my no-show at the Honcho's office. Despite the fact that it wasn't actually my fault. Frankie had failed to hold the Honcho's attention for more than one minute flat – then the Honcho had pitched him out. Resulting in Operation Mad Dog. Luckily the Honcho hadn't locked his door so Frankie had nipped back in.

'So? Did you get any info? Anything on Heath? Lauren? Or ... the staff?'

'Not a thing.'

'*Whaa*? You're kidding me! Nothing?'

Had Frankie missed the whole point of this operation? Information on the others was just pure nosiness, but information on the staff was what I really needed. Someone in this place knew everything I needed to know and yet Frankie was just standing there grinning at me, his head crooked like one of those crazy meerkats on TV.

The ground of the old cottage had flooded in the earlier rain and the place smelled damper than ever. The sun outside had returned for a while, but now it was sliding away again. Daytime turning to night.

I walked outside, then turned to face him as he came bounding out after me.

'So what am I doing all the way out here if you've got nothing to tell me?' I asked.

'Because, Ben Parker, *Nosy* Parker, you're going to give me some information first. Remember? Scratch my back and I'll scratch yours?'

'Yeah, yeah, I got that, Frank. I'm gonna put in a

word for you with Lauren, remember?'

'Sure, but we both know that's not going to work. Lauren doesn't like me that way, and nothing you can say will change that. No, I've decided I'm more interested in you, Bennie Boy.'

Now this was *way* out of my league!

'Er, Frankie, I erm, you know, get on with you okay now and that, but erm, no, this isn't for me. I like girls. *Really* like them, in fact. I'm–I'm flattered but like … no thanks.'

'What the frig are you on about? I don't *fancy* you, you prat! I wanna know why you're *in* here. What's the story, kiddo?'

The relief literally blew out of my nostrils. Frankie and Bennie as a couple – *Frannie* – was just not something I even wanted to consider.

'What do you mean? I'm in here cos I'm "troubled". Like everyone else.'

'Bullshit. We're all in here cos we wanna be here. Well, you, me and Lauren anyway.'

Who told him? Lauren? Did Allie tell her that? Or had she overheard me tell Allie?

'You're just like us, Ben. Now spill!'

He followed me down to the edge of the water where I took my shoes off and paddled in. He stood there, waiting on my confession. It was one of those moments where you can't go forwards until you go backwards. I looked down at my wet feet and the shore water shimmering over them and thought, what the hell? He could help me.

So I told him. Told him all about being adopted and how I was determined to find out who I really was.

'So you're looking for your *ma*? In *here*?'

Frankie's face was screwed up like a newborn Labrador.

'Yeah, well, maybe not *in* here, but Mum's social-worker friend told me I might find *something* here. She was the one who showed me a picture of the place in the *Telegraph*. Then I left it where Dad could see it and he took the bait.'

'And your mum and dad, the ones you grew up with, they don't know anything about this?'

'No. Helen – Mum's work colleague – said it was a secret. Said she knew things from back in the old days when she worked for the adoption agency. I suppose she didn't want me upsetting Mum any more than I usually did.'

'Jesus, and I thought *I* operated outside the law!' he said, scratching his thick red hair.

'Helen's not operating outside the law. Not really. She's just trying to help.'

He looked at me then like I was a lift that didn't

go all the way to the top. In fact, the way he usually looked at me.

'Whatever you say, Bennie Boy, but it sounds sus to me. Hang on a minute – what did you say her name was? The social worker?'

'Helen. Helen Crawford. She works in the same department as my mum. My *adoptive* mum.'

'Crawford?' he said, chewing over the word like it was gristle. 'Helen Crawford?' Frank was reaching into the recesses of his brain for something. I knew this because when he thought about something really hard he scratched his head even more. 'That was the name of *my* social worker. The new one. The one I was changed to after the joyriding. Skinny woman with a big nose?' He looked around at me like he'd just discovered gravity. 'Hey, she told *me* to come here too!'

Okay, so that was a bit of a freaky coincidence, but Helen seemed to be that sort of person. She was probably just trying to sort Frankie out like she was me. Or was she? I swatted my suspicions away like flies. For now.

'Anyway, I've told you what you wanted to know,' I said. 'Now spill the beans on what you really found on the Honcho's computer.'

'But don't you think that's weird?'

'Yeah, yeah, so we both know the same social

worker. Norn Iron is a small place, Frankie. No big deal. Come on, you can't have hacked into Wilson's computer and seen nothing! *Spill!*'

His eyes were still a bit glazed over at this big coincidence he'd discovered, but a shake of his head seemed to pull him back to the here and now.

'Nothing much. I didn't have time. A few addresses, that's all.'

'Whose?'

'Allie Cooper has an address in Comber – but Lauren already told me that. She has a small house there that she inherited from some relation. She used to live there full-time before she got the live-in job in Knockmore House. Strange but Chris has a place in Comber too. Didn't have time to look at his info properly though.'

'Lauren certainly has her sources, like she said.'

'Yeah – you know what she told me? Wilson was married once. No children. His wife left him. I wonder why?'

'The comb-over, I'd say.'

I don't know what I'd expected him to find. The words '**Ben Parker's Mother Was Here**' were hardly going to flash up like an advertisement. My fault. I should have asked him to search for the surname Rogan. Or Simon Street. Helen had shown me – just for a few moments – a scrap of paper with *Simon*

Street written on it, copied underneath in a child's crayon scrawl. She had made no comment as I stared at it. It had taken my breath away and sent shivers up my spine. Was I the child who had written that? And now it turned out that half of the *inmates* here seemed to come from Simon Street anyway. Jesus, maybe I was related to Frankie? Or worse, maybe I was related to Lauren! I began to think I would have to get on that computer myself.

'Right, Frank, next time it's my turn. I do the hacking – you do the distracting.'

'You didn't do any distracting this time!'

'Yeah, yeah. Sorry about that.'

He was scratching his head again.

'Seriously, Frank, go and ask for some Hedrin. You're making me start to bloody scratch now too!'

Chapter thirteen

Sunday morning dawned as fresh as dew and I was seriously glad that we were all getting the morning off. Those who wanted to go to church were mini-bused into Comber – the rest of us could just lie around and watch telly.

I had just settled myself into position on the L-shaped sofa in the TV room when the Honcho appeared.

'Tomorrow morning, Ben. Your family will be here around eleven o'clock.'

He looked pleased with himself, as if he'd gone out of his way to arrange a family visit when it was actually routine.

I wasn't so sure I even wanted to see them. Amy

yes – Mum and Dad, no.

'It's a week since they brought you here, Ben. I'm sure they'll see a big change in you.'

'They will?' I asked. It was no good – I had kept my sarcasm in check for long enough with this guy. 'Yeah, I suppose. I've grown a beard since they last saw me and I've found my inner animal.'

He sighed one of those sighs that adults use when they're trying to be really patient, but actually they want to clip you round the head.

'Don't you want to heal yourself, Ben?' he asked.

'Heal myself? I'm not a bloody leper!'

'Of course you're not, Ben, but you're an angry young man who needs to think about people other than himself. Your family are suffering too, Ben. Give them a bit of a break, eh?'

Why did everyone in here think I was just a selfish prig? Maybe somebody could consider *my* feelings for a change?

'Go on, enjoy your day off. You're off duty tomorrow morning too so you can take some time to prepare yourself. And think on this, Ben – this isn't just about you.'

Bloody right it wasn't. It was about somebody called Rogan who owed me a big explanation! I lay around watching *Love Island* on catch-up and actually started to miss the rest of the gang. Lauren and Frank had gone to Mass and some of the others had gone to services in their own churches. I was beginning to regret not tagging along myself. My gran was a great believer in lighting candles – maybe a holy candle or two might just have done the trick. But then – there *were* matches involved in that.

I stood at my bedroom window that night, listening to the huge, dark sounds of the farm. I opened up my hands and saw a map of lines running through my palms. Like valleys. What would Frankie Boy say if he saw me now, staring at my hands like a flippin' maniac? But these lines, these marks, they came from somewhere. From someone. Who did I inherit them from?

The day Mum and Dad told me the truth I ran and ran until I thought I was going to burst. I slumped to the ground behind a Tesco Express and knuckled my eyes like a wee kid, sobbing myself dry. I knew kids in school who were adopted and it never seemed to affect them. Maybe they knew from the beginning. Maybe they were putting on a performance. I was full of rage and self-pity that night and I was determined to punish someone.

Now I lay down on the bed and stared at the ceiling, hoping for inspiration. I tried so hard to unwrap it all. Why did Helen tell me to come here? What was the connection between this place and my mother? And what about the *Simon Street* scrap of paper? Sometimes you just know that your life is about to change. There were things said and unsaid, spaces in the past that I just couldn't get my head round. My head started to pound just puzzling it all out. I decided I would put it to my *parents* the next day – it was time they told me some truth.

Chapter fourteen

The next day Amy burst out of the car and ran to me like I was her long-lost brother. Which I was. In a way.

'Hi there, Ames,' I said, giving her a big cuddle. 'How's life back at the serpentarium?'

'Okay. I've got a new snake but she's not as cute as Sindy.'

'Look, I'm really sorry about Sindy, Ames. I'm an idiot. That notion of doing a breakdance act with her was plain stupid. I mean, the guy I saw on Youtube was dancing with a cobra – not a wee corn snake. But, trampling on her … that was just wrong.'

I wasn't being truthful with her and I felt bad. The whole point of doing the snake dance was to add another thing to my list of 'misdemeanours'. But hurting Sindy wasn't part of my plan.

'It's okay,' Ames said, cuddling into me again. 'But it *was* kinda dumb.'

'Yeah, well, your big brother does a lot of dumb things, Ames. You'll have to get used to that.'

'Or maybe she could have a big brother who learns from his mistakes, Ben?'

It was Mum, using her social-worker voice and talking down to me like I was her client or something.

'Hi, Mum.'

'Hello, love,' she said. 'We've missed you.'

Dad just kicked at a stone on the ground and nodded his head while Mum did the tactile bit.

'We've downloaded all your favourite programmes so you can watch them when you come home,' Mum said.

For a minute I couldn't even remember what my favourite programmes were. Or whether I'd even want to watch them.

'And Gran says hello. Says you've got to eat plenty of protein and build yourself up.'

My gran had some fixation about me 'building myself up'. I wasn't exactly a weed but, boy, did she make me feel like one!

'Come on then,' said Mum. 'Let's go inside.'

She tried to put her arm around my shoulder but I was having none of it. I shrugged it away and walked with Amy instead. Dad followed behind.

Kate Bridges ushered us in, Knockmore Smile in place, and told us to use the Family Room because of its *ambience*. To me it was just more cream walls and sick-inducing pictures of 'happy' families.

'There are no pictures of snakes in here,' complained Amy.

'I know, Ames, but reptiles aren't really the look they're going for.'

'Well, they should. Mum, can I get some paper?'

'Go on, love,' Mum answered, nodding at paper and felt-tips on a table in the far corner. Apparently drawing was part of their master-therapy in here.

While Amy was doodling away at the other end of the room, Mum put me through the inquisition.

'So how have you been? Have you settled in? Made any new friends? What's it like working with the animals?'

'Which question do you want me to answer first, Mum?' I asked her sarcastically.

'You're right, love. Just tell us what you want to tell us.'

She was really trying, I could see that, but I still wasn't ready to give her a break. She wasn't wearing any make-up and I had to admit to myself that she looked pretty rough. Mum was one of those women who always wore make-up, even just to pop out to the shops. She kept herself in good nick – at least that's what Dad always said when he wasn't complaining about the money she spent every month on her hair. Apparently that 'sun-kissed' look didn't come cheap anymore.

'Talk to your mother, son. She's been worried about you,' Dad said in a low voice.

I looked at Dad with as much venom as I could muster.

'I would love to talk to my mother, but I don't know where she is or even *who* she is!'

'Now, Ben, that's uncalled for,' he said, trying to keep his voice down and glancing at Amy. 'Your mother is right in front of you and you know it. Stop being so insensitive.'

'Insensitive? *Insensitive*? Telling me that I'm a waif on the day of my fourteenth birthday is insensitive!'

He turned and looked out through the window and Mum put her head in her hands. I knew they wanted a happy, warm visit, but hey! You don't always get what you want, do you?

Amy marched back over with an armful of paper and proceeded to tell us off.

'Come on, you lot. Mum, Dad – you promised you wouldn't argue with Ben.'

'I know, Amy, but it's very hard not to argue with your brother,' Dad mumbled back.

'She's right, Colin. Let's start again.' Mum the mediator, trying to fix us like she always does. 'We don't have to talk about the farm, Ben, if you don't want to.'

'Okay. Let's talk about where I came from then.'

'We've been through this before, Ben,' she said. 'We don't know anything. All we know is that when we saw you for the first time we loved you. And we still do. Isn't that enough?'

I looked at Amy with her wee eyes all glazing up with tears and decided to tread a bit more carefully. She knew all about my adoption, but I didn't want her to feel screwed-up about it. Like I did.

I told her to go back to the table and draw the fiercest snake she could imagine, then I leaned forward towards Mum and lowered my voice.

'So how come Helen knows then?'

Mum looked thrown.

'Helen? Helen who?'

'Helen Crawford, who used to work with you!' I seethed. 'How come she knows all about me and you two don't?'

I hadn't planned to tell them about Helen, but a week of brooding in here had made me finally come out with it. Hell, what did I have to lose?

Mum's jaw was slowly dropping and the pupils in her eyes were turning into planets. She looked at Dad, whose jaw had dropped even lower than hers.

'What are you talking about, Ben?' she finally said.

'I'm talking about Helen Crawford,' I said slowly. 'Now come on. *Spill!*'

Mum was shaking her head and screwing up her forehead now. She actually looked totally confused.

'Seriously, Ben, I really don't know what you're talking about. What has Helen Crawford got to do with this?'

'She told me I'd find something out about my birth mother here.'

'She *what*?' Dad spluttered.

'Helen told me about Knockmore in the first place,' I explained. 'She said there was some kind of connection and I'd find out what I needed to know.'

Mum and Dad were looking at each other as if someone was about to get murdered. Then Mum started to do this weird trembling thing and Dad put his arms around her.

'Calm down, Claire. Take a deep breath. We can fix this,' he was saying.

'Fix what? *Me*?' I interrupted.

'No, Ben, believe it or not, not *everything* in life is about you!'

He turned back to Mum and rubbed her back, speaking softly to her which wasn't really Dad's thing. Amy ran back over and climbed up on Mum's knee and gave her a hug and I thought: so this is what it's going to be like – me on the outside looking in.

'Ben,' said Dad, 'when did Helen Crawford tell you all this? Try and remember.'

He was being all Master and Commander now which spooked me a bit. I was beginning to wish I hadn't mentioned Helen Crawford. I'd obviously hit a nerve.

'Ben, talk to us. When and where did Helen speak to you?'

'I don't know, a month ago maybe. She was waiting outside of school one day, said she wanted to help but she didn't want to worry you two. Told me not to say anything.' And showed me the scrap of paper with the crayon "clue".

'I'll bet she did!' said Dad through gritted teeth.

Mum was rocking back and forwards and shaking her head.

'Why? What's so wrong with that?' I asked. I was starting to feel a bit weird. 'She was only trying to help. Wasn't she?'

'Oh yeah, Helen's been very helpful!' laughed Dad. A harsh, strange sort of laugh. 'Since she was struck off, she's done her level best to upset your mum. The woman's a walking nightmare.'

'What do you mean – struck off?' I asked, feeling a bit like rocking back and forth myself.

'It means she had to step down from her role as a social worker, Ben,' Mum said. 'I discovered that some of her practices were – well, inappropriate. I didn't want to say anything – I've known Helen for years. But what she was doing was wrong. I had to do something.'

She burst into tears, crying out loud which wasn't something she did very often. I wanted to make her better right then, I really did. But I just couldn't.

'Helen was selling false information to people about their birth parents,' said Dad. 'Among other things. Your mum was duty bound to inform her line manager. Somehow Helen found out that your mum was responsible and she's been making her life hell ever since. Tried to get her sacked. And now this.' He shook his head. 'It all makes sense now.'

'False information?'

'Yes, Ben, *false* information,' said Mum. 'I'm sorry, love, but she's just used you to get at me. There's probably nothing at Knockmore that connects you to your birth, love. It's all a lie.'

She unwrapped Amy from her shoulders and came and held me. For a long time. And then Dad held me too, and we rocked back and forth together. Until the shadow of our heads merged into the wall. And for a moment – just a moment – I forgot to hate them. My mum and dad. The same mum and dad who took me to the hospital when I was nine after I'd swallowed a rubber in school for a bet. The same mum and dad who taught me how to ride my bike without stabilisers when I was five. The same mum and dad who were impostors and had lied to me for most of my life. What the hell was I supposed to think now?

Dad looked at me then and I swear there was so much pain in those eyes I felt like I had pierced him through the heart. Maybe it *was* time to give my family a break.

Chapter fifteen

'So how did the visit go, Ben?'

I was back in my room when Allie knocked at the door. My head was reeling from what Mum and Dad had told me, and to be honest I didn't know what to believe.

'Okay,' I answered. 'Mum and Dad were a bit upset though. Well, a *lot* upset.'

'Parents often find their first visit overwhelming. They'll get used to it.'

'No, they weren't upset about visiting,' I explained. 'It was about something I told them. Something about finding my real mother.'

Allie did that thing with her eyes again, looking right through me as if I were glass.

'Why is that so important to you, Ben? Finding your birth mother? What if she doesn't want to be found? What if she's no longer around?'

'Well, she bloody well should be!' I said. 'I have, like, six million questions I want to ask her!'

'And what if you don't like the answers, Ben? Or what if she simply doesn't have any? You've got to put this fairy-tale notion out of your head that it will be a wonderful reunion with hearts and kisses. It mightn't be like that at all, you know. Your mum might not even be alive!'

'Why are you saying that? Why is everyone so bloody determined to keep the truth from me?'

She blew her choppy fringe away and looked past me to the fields outside. Her hair wasn't sun-kissed like Mum's, just regular brown, but it shone like Sky's saddle. She sat there for about five minutes, saying nothing, as if she were lost in a book.

'The truth?' she finally said. 'The truth is your mother and your father could no longer give you what you needed. It's possible that they're not even around anymore. Instead you found a loving home and a good life. Why are you so intent on spoiling all that? What you're looking for may not be out there.'

Why was she being so negative? I just wanted to know who I *was* – what could be so bad about that?

'Did you enjoy seeing Amy?' she asked.

'Yeah, course I did. What did you ask me that for?'

No answer. Just that intense stare. Why was she always questioning me about Amy? Did she think I had some sort of hang-up about her? Because I didn't – I really didn't. I was the age Amy is now when they told me there was a baby coming. Mum was swelling out of her clothes with a bump under her skin and I wanted to know why she seemed to be getting bigger and bigger. They hadn't told me sooner cos they thought they'd lose it. I remember thinking that Mum wasn't that careless – she never lost *anything*. It was always Dad who misplaced things. How could you misplace a baby? Dad used funny words like *foetus* and *embryo* and told me how excited he was. And the truth is – I was too. And when she arrived into the world I used to love to watch her sleep. Her little mouth hanging open, her chest rising and falling, her wee Babygro clinging to her soft skin. If Allie thought I hated my little sister, she couldn't have been more wrong – I loved her.

'I'd like you to work with Heath this afternoon,' Allie was saying, changing the subject again. 'He needs some company. He needs *your* company.'

'Heath needs *my* company? For what?' I asked, sneering at her like she was an imbecile.

'It's the anniversary of his parents' death in the accident today,' she said, looking away. 'He comes here every year around this time. Heath has no parents to speak of, Ben. You do. Count yourself lucky.'

And she was gone. Mercury quick – out the door and away. And *I* was supposed to cheer up Silent Boy. Bloody great!

'Alright, Heath? What's our duty today then?' I asked him, trying to get myself into role as some kind of 'company' facilitator.

He pointed towards the stables.

'Mucking out?' I asked. 'Okay then,' I sighed. 'Let's do it.'

I was kind of looking forward to seeing Sky again, but when we reached the stables she was already out.

'Allie took her,' said one of the other boys. 'Took off on her like a bat out of hell. She seemed sort of upset.'

I couldn't imagine Allie racing on Sky like that, but then again everyone around here was turning out to be a bit unpredictable. Lauren hadn't smiled a smile or spoken a word to anyone in two days. And now apparently Heath wanted company – Martha the Sow would fly next!

There were two horses waiting to be groomed so Heathcliff and I set to work. He looked easy around the horses. Happy even.

'Woah there, boy!' I yelped. 'Keep your bloody head away from my privates!'

Dury, a grey pony, seemed to have taken a liking to my inside leg. I'd been warned about this one. Heath was looking after a dark-brown cob called Bobby who was about as silent as he was. In fact, it even looked a bit like him. Heath handed me something called a dandy brush and I got stuck into taking as much mud off Dury's body as I could. We'd been told that if the horses didn't get a brush down every day then dried muck could rub under their girth and cause sores. I don't know why, but the thought of the horses having sores sort of angered me. There was something about these horses that was getting to me. They kind of made me forget. When I looked over at Heath I knew that they were having the same effect on him.

'He seems to like that, Heath.'

Heath was brushing Bobby's mane. Slowly and carefully, just the way he did everything in fact. He moved on to the tail, taking the tangles out as if it were a child's hair.

'If a job's worth doing …'

Shit! Did Heath just say that? Did he just *speak*? I

117

didn't see his lips move but I could have sworn I heard those words. I looked around to see if there was anyone else with us. But there was no-one.

'Heath? Did you … did you just *say* something?'

Slowly he turned his head, looked at me. Then nodded. He *had* spoken! To me!

'*You can speak!*' I squeaked.

'Yeah, course I can speak. I just save it for when I have something to say.'

His voice was gravelly, but sort of musical.

'But, but, like, when was the last time you did? Speak, I mean?'

'Dunno. Few months ago maybe,' he shrugged.

He was still untangling knots in Bobby's tail, as if nothing out of the ordinary had just happened. Meanwhile I stood there with my jaw hanging down like a ventriloquist's dummy.

'So, why don't you talk the rest of the time?'

Silence. Just the scraping of a comb through hair.

'Heath?'

'Nothing to talk about.'

Four more words. I was getting somewhere.

'I heard today's a tough day for you,' I went on. 'It really sucks – what happened to you, I mean.'

His face clouded for a minute. Maybe I had pushed him too far.

'Yeah,' he answered. 'It does. I come here to forget.'

So another volunteer to Knockmore. Did anyone actually get sent here against their will?

'This place helps then?' I asked, treading carefully.

'Sort of. Kind of puts the world the right way up again.'

I thought about the previous night when Heath and Chris had played cards together. No talking. Just being together. And the night before that when Allie had talked for hours to Erin Freeman about her diabetes. And it actually seemed to help because Allie understood how Erin felt because she was a diabetic too. They had grouched for ages about how crap it was having to inject themselves, like four times a day. Maybe this place *could* heal.

Heath looked up at me, sort of studying me for a minute, like he was thinking of saying more. He looked tired, heavy as stone. But he didn't speak.

In fact, he said nothing more for two whole days. And when he did speak again, it was like the sound of gunshot in my ears. Words that made us all sit up and take notice.

Chapter sixteen

'What's up with Lauren?' I muttered to Frank at dinner.

Her eyes were like two red cherries and she seemed to have even less appetite than usual, pushing the food around her plate with her fork. Heath got up and went to sit beside her. He didn't say anything (of course!). He just sat there and she seemed to thaw out a bit somehow. Those two seemed to get each other and I really wanted to know why.

'Girls are always moody like that,' Frank, the font of all wisdom, mumbled back.

But it wasn't a mood she was in – it was more like a trauma. And I wanted to help but as usual I didn't know how.

'Wanna do some hacking tonight?' Frank muttered.

'Yeah. But I do it this time.'

'Okay, Bennie Boy – let's see how smart you are.'

'So how do we get the Honcho out of his office again?'

'Easy. We tell him the mad dog's back. He knows I was attacked by a half-starved German Shepherd once and that I have *issues* with dogs. And anyway, there's that much guff on the news at the minute about savage dogs that he's paranoid about them.'

'Okay. So where are you going to spot the rabid dog this time?'

'Out front – on the drive. It'll get him right out of the building. Then I can just tell him it must have run off.'

'Well, keep him out there long enough for me to have a good poke around.'

Frankie gave me the thumbs-up, while still gripping his knife and fork, like we'd just come up with some kind of master plan.

'By the way, Heath *spoke* to me this afternoon,' I said, not entirely sure that I should share this.

Frankie cocked one eye up at me as if asking for more information. He wasn't about to take time out of eating to actually use his mouth to ask. I had never met anyone who was as much in love with food as Frankie, yet he was as skinny as a rake. He chewed, chomped and sloshed every mouthful around like today was his last day on earth.

'Yeah, he mentioned the accident,' I said, pleased all of a sudden to be the one imparting information – for a change.

'Rough!' Frankie answered.

'Lauren seems to get on well with him,' I said.

'Lauren gets on well with any lost cause. That's just the way she is,' Frankie said. 'Same as her ma.'

'You know her mum?'

'Knew her, yeah. Years ago, before I left Simon Street.'

'Why did you leave?'

'No-one to look after me properly. I had half a chance when oul' Joe was around. He used to pop in and keep my da right. After he died, well, Da just didn't know how to be a parent. I was taken into care.'

A bowl of apple-pie and ice cream was set down in front of him and I knew I had no chance of getting anything more out of him now. And there was me, a well-off kid in a well-off corner of Belfast living the suburban lifestyle and thinking *my* life was a crock of shit. I had always got everything I wanted: best trainers, best gadgets, you name it and it was there. I was so freakin' lucky. But I was so freakin' lost.

Lauren didn't speak at Circle Time and Chris the Priss didn't push her. Obviously I was the only one around here not allowed to remain silent. He blathered on about camaraderie and friendship and how each of us could help the others, which I thought was a total load of crap. The things that had happened to Heath and Frankie – and possibly Lauren – were not going to be fixed by gossiping with someone like me while shovelling shit. But what did I know? Lauren was fiddling with her pink stone and just staring into the distance. Sometimes her eyes seemed to change colour – they were always blue, but at times they were powder-blue and at other times like tonight they were like steel. I knew this because I was staring straight at them.

'Ben? Anything you wish to share?' asked Chris, taking his baseball cap off for once.

I hadn't forgiven him for his first interrogation but I was damned if I was going to let him see that he bothered me.

'Yeah,' I said. 'That Sky is one cool horse!'

He raised one eyebrow ever so slightly, waiting for a smart-ass comment. I didn't give him one.

'She spooks easily, nervous, but she's solid as stone underneath,' I said.

'I'm glad you've found something you like on the farm,' said Chris, still waiting for me to sidestep him somehow. 'Sky's been through a lot. She needs careful handling. That's why Allie spends a lot of time with her.'

Was it my imagination or did he seem to soften a bit when he mentioned Allie?

'Do you think I'll be allowed to ride her?' I asked.

'Not until you're ready. And when Sky is ready too.' It was Allie's voice this time. She looked sort of windswept as she walked into the room. 'I've been out on her all afternoon and she still needs coaxing. Cajoling. When the time is right though, I'll let you know. In the meantime you could always ride Dury or Bobby.'

Don't know why but I was kind of excited about that. Dury was only a pony but he was strong enough and I had to start somewhere.

Some movement seemed to catch the corner of Allie's eye. She looked towards Heath and nodded.

'Yes, you too, Heath. I haven't forgotten you want to ride.'

For the first time that evening Lauren looked like she'd come back to us. Her eyes lit up the room as she smiled at Allie. 'Hey – you're not going to forget me, are you?'

'No,' laughed Allie. 'How could I ever forget *you*, Lauren?'

I suddenly realised we were all smiling. Everyone in the room. Even Heath. The light was beginning to fade outside but inside we were all sort of ablaze. Vibrant even. Knockmore was one weird kinda place!

Chapter seventeen

The Honcho was rifling through some papers when I peeped through the door. He had lines across his forehead like he was worried about something. Really worried.

'Mr Wilson?' I coughed. 'I think you better get outside. Frankie's having a meltdown.'

'What's wrong with that boy now?' he said, not even looking up at me.

Right on cue Frankie started yowling and yelping like a demented hyena. The Honcho looked up, panic spreading across his face. He pushed past me and ran out into the corridor but then turned back, bundled me out the door and locked it behind him.

Crap! How was I going to get into his office now?

I darted along the corridor, checking that he was out of sight. Then I remembered the top part of his office window had been open.

I ran around the corner, got up on the windowsill and squeezed my way in, grazing my back in the process. I fell head first on to the floor. *Shit!* Someone was bound to hear me, crying out like a baby without its dummy. I waited. Nothing. No-one.

Then I saw the papers on his desk, the ones he'd been scratching his head about five minutes earlier. I scuffled through them like a rat on night duty searching through detritus. There were numbers and more numbers and pound signs and zeros. A *lot* of zeros! None of it made any sense to me, until I saw the words **'under-subscribed'**. I read on: **'Spare capacity – half of places unfilled. Not viable.'** I wasn't always the sharpest tool in the shed, but even I knew this meant Knockmore was in trouble. Right enough, I had noticed that not one of us had to share a room. And the luxury around here! It must have cost a fortune! So how come they couldn't attract other 'yobs with probs' like us? Too expensive? But then, how did Frankie's people pay? And Lauren's? And all the others? I knew Mum and Dad had decided to forgo a family holiday this summer to pay for my *confinement*.

Footsteps approached the door.

Crikey!

It didn't sound like a man though.

I tried to shuffle the papers back into some kind of order.

A knock on the door.

'John?'

Shit! I hid down on the floor behind his desk. The next thing a key turned in the lock. The door opened.

Silence. Someone looking around the room. I tried to hold my breath like the time Mum took Amy and me to Lisburn Swimming Pool. I had lasted fifteen seconds then. But how long would I last now?

'For God's sake!' a female voice muttered. 'You said you'd be here!'

It wasn't Allie or any of the other voices I'd come to recognise at Knockmore. But I *did* recognise it from somewhere. Then I heard the Honcho's voice and I nearly wet myself.

'Helen! I'm here – just had a little issue to sort out. Tell you what – let's get out of here. I've had enough for one day with mad dogs and crazy kids. It's what – five thirty? Fancy a drink?'

Helen! It couldn't be. *Could* it?

'Okay – I could do with a wine or three,' she answered. 'King's Arms?'

'No – farther afield,' he muttered. 'I don't want the staff to see us talking together. Not out of hours.'

I heard footsteps cross the room and the window shutting, then more footsteps and the sound of the key turning in the lock. I breathed again – hard, heavy, gulping breaths. I was left to my own devices now – a whole night of searching lay ahead, undisturbed.

I scrambled up to the computer and keyed in the word 'password'. Nothing. I tried again. I tried upper case, lower case, I tried the word in reverse order. Nothing. Had Frankie been telling me the truth?

'Ben? Are you in there?'

It was Frankie. He was attempting a whisper from the other side of the door but instead it came out like a smoker's rasp.

'Let me in!' he wheezed.

'I can't! The door's locked.'

'Open the window then!'

Would you believe it? The window was bloody well locked now too! I searched around for one of those cylinder-shaped gold keys that are used for windows. Mum usually left ours lying around on the sill somewhere. I ran my hands along the top of cabinets and cupboards. I looked in drawers, on the floor, everywhere. *Crap!* I was locked in here! Old

Wilson was so concerned about security he'd locked everything.

But luckily hadn't shut the computer down.

'I can't get out, Frankie. I'm stuck!'

'Great! Then you've got all night to look.'

'How can I look if I don't know the password? You gave me the wrong one!'

'I didn't. He must have changed it.'

Why would he have changed the password just now? Coincidence? Or had he somehow copped that Frankie – or someone else – had been messing with the computer?

'Try … try Knockmore or Wilson or – or something,' Frankie was saying.

'You're some help!' I seethed.

I tried every possible combination of words I could think of – backwards and forwards. Then it hit me. *Nendrum*. I typed it in and – *bingo!* Suddenly everything loaded up in front of me.

What was the story with the Honcho and Helen Crawford? It couldn't be a relationship, could it? Anyway, that piece of juicy detail was for later. Right now I wanted to find out what Knockmore had in store for *me*.

I didn't know what I was going to find. I could feel my stomach tighten the way it does before a maths exam or a football match. My throat was as dry as tinder and my hands felt clammy.

I typed in '**Ben Parker**' and waited. Date of birth, home address, behavioural issues, school report – nothing really of any interest. I saw the words '**Victim Mentality Disorder**' and '**Passive Aggressive**' and thought, yeah, that's right, give me a label, why don't you?

'Find anything?' Frankie asked from the other side of the door.

'Not yet.'

'Well, I'm off to bed then. Enjoy your night of luxury.'

I looked around me. There wasn't a sofa or anything in the office or even an armchair. It looked like my bed for the night was the cold green carpet on the floor.

'Gee, thanks, Frank. Don't worry about me or anything!'

'I won't!' came the reply.

I rifled through staff details and found one or two surprises. Then I moved on to the *troubled teens* and scrolled down to Parker, Ben. There were reports from Mum and Dad about my recent behaviour. Then there was a statement from Gran. '**Ben's not the boy I thought he was,**' it said. Boy, was that ironic! Good old Gran – always sharp as a tack. I laughed out loud in spite of myself. Then my school report was tagged in there too – plenty of '**Bright boy but does not work hard enough**' sort of thing.

And then I saw two sentences, riddled with spelling mistakes, with Amy Parker typed at the bottom of it.

'**Ben is my big bruther but he's sad becos he dosnt want to be in or family any more. I'm sad to becos I think Im going to loose him.**'

My stomach cramped. I wanted to fly through the window, burst through the walls of our home, break down the door and tell her: I will *always* be your brother.

In the end I didn't. I lay down on the floor and slept and dreamt of wild horses chasing me until I couldn't catch my breath. Their hooves thudding behind me. Their wild fringed eyes haunting me. I lay there until the cleaner unlocked the door the next morning.

Chapter eighteen

The cleaner was singing and swaying as she came in, wearing earphones and more or less oblivious to all around her. She didn't look much older than me. I shook myself out of a fitful sleep and crawled around the Honcho's desk. In a split second I was out of there. Undetected and unscathed. Sort of.

'Ben? You're up early!'

Crap! It was Allie Cooper. She was coming out of the staff kitchen.

'Er, yeah, just felt like an early-morning walk,' I said.

'Really? You look like you haven't been to bed!'

'Erm, I always look like this in the morning.'

She raised one eyebrow at me the way my dad does when he doesn't believe a single word I'm saying.

'You know what, Ben – I haven't really got time to go into this right now, but we *will* talk about it later. Now go and get an hour's rest before breakfast. We're all heading out for the day. That's why I've come downstairs early – to get some paperwork done before we head off.'

'We're going out?'

'Yep, John Wilson texted me this morning. Said we're all to assemble in the foyer at eight. Staff, students, everyone.'

'Why?' I asked.

She shrugged her shoulders. 'I suppose he just thinks we all need a day off. The minibuses will pick us up at the front door. Make sure you're wearing suitable footwear. Knowing John, there'll be lots of walking involved.'

By eight we were all assembled like sixteen primary-school kids heading to the zoo. Lauren looked *way* better. In fact, she looked gorgeous! Her long hair was wound up in some scrunchie thing on top of her head but wisps of it were escaping and hanging down like spider silk.

'Do you know where we're going?' I asked her.

'Nendrum, I think. Then maybe out on the lough.'

'*In a boat?*' I squeaked. (Why did I always squeak when I was around her?) 'In a boat?' I said again, reaching down into my larynx for the deepest, most guttural sound I could make. This time it sounded like a Strangford foghorn.

'Yeah, in a boat,' she said, looking at me oddly.

'Cool,' I said, shrugging my shoulders like I went out boating every day. In the middle of a lough. Forty metres deep. Where the water was so dark and deep it looked as black as oil.

We loaded onto the minibuses and drove just a couple of miles to Nendrum where we jumped off like a rabble of city kids who'd never seen the countryside. Only Heath took his time and walked quietly in the opposite direction from everyone else.

'You been here before?' I asked Lauren, munching on an egg-and-onion sandwich that had been packed for lunch later on. I was turning into a compulsive eater like Frankie.

'Yeah, Allie brought me here on my first day. Quiet, isn't it? Sort of, I don't know, spiritual.'

'Hard to believe that this place was buzzing with monks in the 400s,' I said, trying to sound intellectual, while doing my best not to choke on raw onion.

We looked around us. There had been orchards, gardens, fields, even a sort of guesthouse here once. All built around the church and round tower.

'You wanna pop into the visitor's centre and find out some more?' I asked her.

'Nah, just want to sit here and soak up the sun.

Sometimes you find things out just by staying still and looking.'

Maybe I should try that, I thought, instead of scrabbling around the Honcho's office in the middle of the night.

She whipped the scrunchie thing off and her hair fell like waves around her shoulders.

I wanted to know her story. I wanted to know why she was here, why she'd been sad lately.

'I was a bit of a prat when I arrived at Knockmore, wasn't I?' I said.

'A *bit*?' she said with a smile. 'I guess we all were. But, you know,' she said, sweeping her arm around the views over the lough, 'you sort of put things in perspective after a while.'

Perspective. That was the word my mum had used. Looking across at the yacht club at Whiterock, I could see it all for a moment as Mum could. A coast of foam and light, she'd called it, with its fibreglass buoys chiming and tinkling in the water. I knew I was lucky. Not just to be here, but to be part of the Parker family.

'My mum's a recovering alcoholic,' Laura said quietly. 'I'm just worried that she might start drinking again while I'm in here. Helen promised me she'd be well looked after …'

Helen? Helen Crawford?

'But … I can't stop worrying. She missed her last visit and I don't know why. It's really bothering me.'

Bloody hell – was Helen Crawford the *only* social worker in Northern Ireland?

'Helen, you said. You mean Helen Crawford?'

'Yes.'

'How come we all know Helen Crawford?' I was thinking out loud.

'Do we? *All* know Helen Crawford?' Lauren asked, turning towards me.

'Well, she signed you in here and Frankie and me – and God knows who else. And last night she was hanging around with the Honcho. Weird, isn't it?'

Lauren just shrugged. 'Don't see why. She's a social worker who deals with teenagers. John Wilson is manager of Knockmore. There's no big mystery.'

But I was sure there was more to it than that.

'You're the one who watches all those old detective shows,' I said. 'Think like that old bloke Columbo. What would he say about the connection?'

She just shrugged again. Then her face grew harder. Her blue eyes looked small. Sore.

'I tell you my mum's an alcoholic and all you can think about are stupid, childish mysteries! You are so up your own …' She shook her head and didn't finish, but I got the message. And she was right. What she had said about her mum had shocked me.

Made me realise how hard her life must be. She'd opened up to me and I didn't make a single comment. Not a single scrap of sympathy.

'Crikey, Lauren, I'm sorry. I–I didn't even realise you'd missed out on a visit.'

She looked at me like I was dirt under her shoe and walked away.

'Lauren. *Lauren*!'

I called after her but it was no use. She was like one of those banshee things my dad's mum used to go on about. She just disappeared into thin air.

'Right, everybody! Group together and follow me!'

It was Chris the Priss, barking orders like he was a sergeant major.

'We're going to walk in the direction of Mahee Castle. There's a little mooring just down the road and Mr Wilson has arranged for four or five boats to be there. We're going to practise some team work, guys.'

I hated the way he said 'guys' like he was in some stupid Australian soap opera.

'*Let's go*!' he shouted.

Frankie was nudging at my shoulder as we walked down the steep bank away from the settlement.

'Well?' he said aggressively. 'When are you going to tell me what you found out last night.'

'I didn't get a chance to tell you,' I said, sounding whiney. 'Allie sent me back to my room this morning. Then I could hardly tell you at breakfast with everyone else around.'

'Well, you're here now. Spill!'

'Truth is, I didn't find very much. Apart from Knockmore being undersubscribed.'

'Under sub-what?'

'They don't have enough *inmates* to match their running costs. They need more yobs. Like us.'

'*I'm no friggin' yob!*' he shouted. 'You calling me names, Bennie Boy?'

'No! I'm just being – you know – ironic. Sarcastic. Taking the piss.'

'Never mind feeding me the dictionary. Tell me more about Knockmore.'

'Well, it looks like it could close down if they don't keep packing it with *troubled teens*.'

'Can't see them having any bother finding those in Belfast!' he scoffed.

'But listen to this – Helen Crawford was there last night. Wanting to talk to the Honcho.'

'What about?'

'Dunno. But he said he didn't want them to be seen together out of hours. Where is he, by the way? Is he meeting us at the boats?'

'Wilson's not here today. Said he was staying

behind to look after the place while we're out and about,' said Frankie.

'But this trip was his idea according to Allie – he was supposed to come with us – take us walking and stuff!'

Had the Honcho wanted rid of us for some reason? Every other member of staff was here – so he'd have Knockmore to himself. Lauren was wrong – this wasn't a stupid, childish mystery. There was definitely something weird going on here and I was determined to suss it out.

'Anyway, any more info? What about the staff? And the inmates? Any goss there?' asked Frank.

'Yeah, bits and pieces. Nothing too mind-blowing. Except,' I said, turning round to him, 'you remember you said Allie Cooper has a house in Comber?'

'Yeah. Killinchy Road.'

'Mmm. Killinchy Road is Chris the Priss's address too. Number 35.'

'Seriously? Bloody hell! I'm sure that's Allie's number!' said Frankie. The penny dropped with a splash into the well. *'Yeuch!'*

'I know,' I said. 'I thought Allie had some taste. What the hell does she see in that prat?'

'Quite a lot as it happens,' said a voice behind. A song-thrush voice.

Chapter nineteen

'So you've been snooping around, boys? Why am I not surprised?'

Her voice was low and breathy. Her choppy fringe fanned out in the breeze.

'I … we … no, you've got it all wrong,' I said pathetically.

'Have I, Ben? Let me guess then, shall I? You and Frank here thought you'd do some investigating on John Wilson's computer. You want to find out about your birth mother and Frank here just wants to find out – anything. Anything he might use as bait in case the occasion arises. Am I right so far?'

There was no point denying it.

'I know it's wrong, Allie, but the social worker

said I'd find answers here. I couldn't stop myself. I just need to know.'

'Which social worker?' she asked.

'Helen Crawford,' I answered, watching her eyes narrowing. 'The one who was at Knockmore last night.'

'Last night? Where did you see her?'

Was it my imagination or were the furrows in her brow getting deeper by the minute?

'At the Honcho's – I mean – at John Wilson's office. Then they left the farm to go and have a talk.'

She stopped walking and stood as still as a corpse. She seemed to be looking into the distance and she wasn't saying a word. I almost checked to see if she was still breathing.

'Allie? You alright?'

'I'm alright, Ben. Just wondering. And thinking.'

I looked at Frankie who just shrugged his shoulders – his default behaviour whenever he was around the female sex. I smelt an opportunity, a chink in Allie's armour. I decided to go for it.

'It's sort of weird, isn't it?' I said. 'You know, the way Helen Crawford signed us all in here: me, Frankie, Lauren and God knows who else.'

I waited. And waited.

'Yes, Ben, it is weird,' she said finally. 'Just like evacuating us all off the site today is weird. But sometimes … sometimes things are better left alone. I've tried telling you that – over and over again, Ben. But you don't listen, do you? No, Ben has to be all-seeing and all-knowing. Do yourself a favour – stop looking! Some things – and people – just don't want to be found.'

I swear her eyes were glazed over. Glassy and unseeing. She left us then, standing there like two scarecrows on a hill. Motionless and noiseless as Nendrum.

'Come on, guys! Into the boats!'

Chris the Priss pulled the throttle and started the motorboat. It was rocking from side to side like a bloody pendulum and I could feel saliva creeping into my mouth as if I was going to retch.

'*Seriously?*' I squeaked at him.

'Seriously!' he said, laughing. 'And now you can show us what you're made of, Mr Parker!'

I could feel myself heaving even before I reached my leg over the side. The bloody thing moved away from the rocks just as I was about to climb aboard and I screamed like a kid on helium.

'Lost your sea legs, Ben?' he grinned.

'Lost them? I never bloody had them!'

'Then this is the chance to overcome your fears, Ben.'

Yeah, whatever!

'Come on, Bennie Boy – you're holding everybody up. Just get into the flippin' boat!' Frankie shouted over the noise of the engine. So much for peace and tranquillity!

I climbed in and crouched down as low as I could while everybody else piled in. There were four to each boat.

The sickly smell of diesel was filling my lungs as the thing thrummed forwards into the water, sea spray splashing everywhere. I vaguely made out Lauren's shape beside me, but mostly I just kept my eyes tightly shut.

'The high seas!' Chris was shouting. *'You can't beat it!'*

Yes, you bloody well could! You could beat it with a dry bed, a soft pillow and no lunatics shouting at you over the drone of an engine that must have been older than the Honcho! The lough rolled under me in giant swells and I felt like I was surrounded by big walls of black water.

'Hey, guys, what's the strongest creature in the sea?' shouted Zach.

Seriously? This was a good time for telling jokes?

'A mussel!' he laughed. Like a maniac.

I wanted to be anywhere – *anywhere* – but in that freakin' boat.

'Look! A curlew!' Chris the Priss was shouting now.

At least I thought that's what he was saying. I opened one eye to see a brownish bird with a long, slender bill like a rapier sitting nearby on a rock, and it was looking at us like we had the brains of a rocking horse! The boat shook and swayed through the water, making my stomach turn with every wave.

But Lauren looked alive. She was facing into the spray like it was the cure for cancer or something, smiling wider than I'd ever seen her. And, believe me, that girl could smile! She was shouting to Chris and the others over the waves, laughing and chatting like she was in a boat every day of her life, talking about travelling across oceans some day when she was older. Strands of hair were streaming across her face like eels. Why the hell was everyone enjoying themselves so much?

Chris was asking us way too many questions about sea life and telling us to work in pairs at bird-spotting, like it was a bloody test.

Then at last the thing started to slow down as we returned to the ruins of the old castle.

I vomited egg and onion all over Chris the Priss as I climbed out.

'Good spin out, guys?' Jack the Lad asked as we entered the castle. Of course, he'd done the sly thing and stayed on dry land instead of taking his life in his hands on a bloody speed boat! 'That wee adventure will put hair on your chests!'

'Er, *no thanks*!' Lauren announced, looking at him with pure disgust.

He led us around the castle which, to be honest, didn't take too long. He told us that it was originally thought that it was built in the sixteenth century but recent excavations had dated it to the late medieval period. Apparently it had been left to rack and ruin until the early 1900's. There wasn't much to see but I could feel that prick of interest that I'd had at Nendrum. Strange that I was so interested in history when I didn't even know my own!

'So, guys – today has been about bonding. Enjoyed yourselves?' Jack the Lad asked.

'Yeah,' I said. 'Chris and I really bonded over my regurgitated sandwich!'

I saw Allie shake her head. Chris the Priss had gone back to Knockmore to clean himself. Vomit was bad enough, but Ben Parker's vomit! I bet he was really happy about that!

'I can't help it if I get seasick!' I said to no-one in particular.

'You can be such a dork!' Lauren mumbled, pushing past me back to the picnic area.

'What? I'm not allowed to throw up?' I asked.

'I'm not talking about throwing up. I'm talking

about you being a sneak. And an insensitive prat. And an all-round first-class cretin!'

Now that was fighting talk! Okay, I could be accused of the first two, but I'm no cretin!

'Give us a break, Lauren. I'm not perfect – none of us are. I'm sorry I seemed insensitive about your mum. Tell me about her.'

And then she did that thing where she just turned herself around. One minute she was a black cloud and the next she was the sun splitting the trees.

'She's the greatest!' she smiled. 'Funny, kind, clever – she's brilliant.'

'Sounds a lot like you,' I said, trying not to sound too nauseating. But I meant it.

'Sometimes things just get too much for her. She can't help it. It's an illness, you know?' she said, looking at me and willing me to agree with her. 'People think it's just weakness, or selfishness, but it's not – it's a disease and she needs help with it. She hasn't had a drink in over a year, but – while I'm in here – who knows?'

'Why *are* you in here?'

'Helen Crawford thought I needed a break from it all,' she said. 'Time to myself. She got Mum to sign the papers and there was nothing I could do about it. It was alright at first, but now … now I just want to go home.'

'You enjoyed yourself today,' I said. 'Out on the boat.'

'Yeah, cos it reminded me of the time Mum and Nana and me took the ferry to Scotland. I like water, I'd love to cross every sea and ocean someday, but right now I want to be home with my mum. I need to see if she's alright.'

'Have you any idea why she didn't visit?' I asked.

'Well, that's the problem. I'm terrified she might be drinking again.'

'But someone would have told you. Taken you aside or something. Wouldn't they?' I asked, putting my arm around her and drawing her towards me. Her hair smelt like sea spray. 'She *can't* be drinking again, Lauren. Allie would have said something. *Somebody* would have said something.'

'Yeah, I know. You're right. It's just that – you always worry, you know? It never goes away.'

Then sobs racked through her so I held her for a long time. And I have to admit, it was nice. Very nice. And very sad.

Chapter twenty

'Right, we're going to find a way for you to see your mum!'

'How?' Lauren asked.

'I don't know yet,' I said. 'But I know somebody who will.'

We were back at Knockmore, stuffing ourselves after a day of walking, sailing, climbing, and every other 'ing' the counsellors could think of. We were knackered. And starving. Except Lauren, of course, who was just pushing the food around on her plate as usual.

'*Frankie, over here!*' I shouted.

'What do yeh want?' he mumbled back with a mouth full of wheaten bread.

'I want your expertise,' I said.

He scrunched up his eyebrows like I was taking the proverbial but it was enough to draw him over.

'What do you want me to do? And how much are you gonna pay me for doing it?' he gobbled, throwing his two legs around a chair and facing us over the back of it.

'Never mind payment, just listen. How do we get Lauren to Simon Street? Just for a few hours?'

'You mean like break out?' he asked, his eyes suddenly full of mischief.

'Not exactly – just leave the premises for a wee while. It's not exactly Fort Knox,' I said. 'No high walls, no locked doors. But how do we get to Simon Street?'

'We go by car,' he said, as if it was the most natural thing in the world. 'We borrow one of the counsellors'. They're around here all day – they won't need it.'

'When you say borrow, Frankie – you mean?'

'I mean *borrow*, Bennie Boy. I can start one of the cars, take it for a ride and bring it back here in one piece. No sweat.'

'No way!' said Lauren. 'I am not joyriding in a car! I might come from Simon Street but I'm no smick!'

'It's the only way to see your mum, to make sure

she's alright,' I said. 'I know it's crazy, but sometimes you have to do what you have to do.'

'He's right, Lauren. I know you've been worried about your mum,' said Frank. 'You've been like a bear with a sore head. If we leave straight after breakfast we can get back here by lunchtime. We'll get someone to cover our duties. Nobody will ever notice.'

'You *think*?' she said. 'Of course they're going to bloody notice!'

'Look, how desperate are you to see her?' I asked. 'Helen Crawford doesn't care about your mum – she's got another agenda. I just haven't figured out what it is yet.'

'He's right,' said Frank. 'And your mum – well, she was good to me when I was a wee fella. Now I wanna return the favour. I know you said your nana keeps an eye on her, but she's not getting any younger, is she?'

'No,' Lauren agreed. 'But – well, we could get in big trouble. And I've *never* been in trouble before. Mum always made sure of that.'

'Well, it's time to make sure your *mum's* not in trouble,' I said.

I could see she was wavering.

'First thing after breakfast then?' I asked.

Her head made the slightest of movements.

Almost a nod, but not quite.

'Tomorrow it is then.'

'Jesus, Frankie! You don't have to let the whole bloody place know that we're stealing a car!' I shouted as he revved at the engine like a maniac.

'Not stealing. *Borrowing*. And I'm just making sure she's warmed up before we hit the road.'

'It's not a bloody motor bike, Frank!' Lauren hissed at him from the passenger seat. 'Now, just get going!'

He took off like a bat out of hell down the long driveway and out through the gates of Knockmore, tearing up the country road like it was a racetrack. I was tossed around the back seat like the *Titanic* as he roared past fields of cows and high hedges.

'*Slow down, Frankie! We want to actually survive this trip!*' I yelled as I desperately struggled to fasten my seat belt.

'It's just the buzz, Bennie Boy. I've missed it. Tearing through the open country like this.'

'*Yeah, in somebody else's car, Frank! Slow down or you'll crash it and kill us at the same time!*' Lauren shouted.

Lauren was panicking and I knew if Frankie didn't slow down she'd change her mind about the whole thing. Luckily Frank must have seen sense –

if he had any – and started to drive at a *relatively* normal pace.

'Who owns this jalopy anyway?' I asked.

'Chris. He hadn't even locked it,' said Frankie. 'Pure cinch!'

Okay, so I had been starting to feel dead guilty – and nervous – about car-jacking, but when I heard it belonged to Chris the Priss I couldn't help but laugh.

I knew I was going to get in a shitload of trouble over this, but something in me really wanted to help Lauren. To put her mind at rest. And that's my whole problem – my *misdemeanours*, as Mum calls them, are usually sparked by the best intentions. Yes, I had deliberately escalated the amount of my petty crimes in order to get into Knockmore, but even before that I normally just sort of got things wrong. Badly wrong sometimes. 'Ill-advised' is what Mum called it (before she began to say it was 'a call for attention'). 'Thoughtless' is what Dad preferred to call it. But today I wasn't being thoughtless. I was trying to help someone in the only way I knew how.

We drove through villages and towns until we hit the Castlereagh Hills and Belfast was in view. There were Samson and Goliath, the two big yellow cranes at Queen's Island, Belfast Lough, Cave Hill – all the places that mapped out my home city. I could see a

Stena Line pushing out through the lough on its way to Scotland. Belfast Castle looked like something out of a miniature fairyland model. I could feel a lump in my throat as I took it all in. Okay, so the truth was that I lived way up in the 'burbs and didn't see these landmarks most of the time anyway, but I realised I missed them. Missed Belfast; missed home. For years Belfast had lost its reason to live – people said it had more past than future. But that wasn't true. Not any more.

But, as Frankie headed north through the city, I realised that I was petrified. Of what, I didn't know – of what Lauren would find? Of getting caught? Of being a passenger in a car driven by Frank Morgan? All I knew was that sweat was trickling down my back and I was starting to feel sick.

'You alright in there?' Lauren asked me. 'You're as green as a bloody kiwi. Aw, don't tell me you get carsick as well as seasick!'

Yep, I sure did! Hadn't thought of that one when I came up with this master plan. Mum always sorted out my travel sickness. Yet another thing I relied on her for. Funny how you notice these things when it's too late.

'Don't worry, Ben. We'll be there soon.'

She gave me one of her smiles but, to be honest, it didn't help.

'If your breakfast comes up all over the back of my head, Bennie Boy – you're dead!' said the ever-thoughtful Frank.

It didn't. But it did come out all over the back seat of Chris the Priss's car. Ah well, silver linings and all that.

Chapter twenty-one

As we drove through narrow, redbrick streets I noticed less and less trees with every corner we turned. Houses ran right along the footpaths and I wondered if the people inside ever felt like they were living in goldfish bowls, moving around in full view like Amy's fish – which she'd so aptly named Finny and Fanny. By now, Lauren's head was so close to the front windscreen I thought she was going to disappear through it.

'Slow down, Frank! Here it is,' she said.

We pulled up alongside Number 42, an end-terrace, and to be honest I was surprised. Two hanging baskets full of flowers hung outside, the front door had a coat of fresh, green paint and the whole place looked pretty cared for.

Lauren was taking deep breaths now and I knew she was panicking.

'What if she's drunk?' she said. 'What if she's hung over and still collapsed in her bed?'

'She won't be,' I said, trying to reassure her, but the truth was I didn't know what we were going to find. The house had an air of calm about it, but who knew what was on the inside?

'Are we going in or not?' Frankie asked, ever the tactful one.

Lauren trembled as if the temperature was sub-zero. Then she did something I'd never seen before. She blessed herself. She closed her eyes and held her hands tight together and didn't speak. Frankie and I eyeballed each other and we knew not to interrupt, not to say anything. After a minute or two I started to feel envious. She was in a place of quietness. And it really seemed to be helping. When she opened her eyes she looked stronger somehow.

'Let's go!' she said and climbed out of the car.

We cowered behind her like Shaggy and Scooby as she unlocked the front door and walked into the house. I could smell polish or Febreze or something familiar. Something that Mum used. We walked down a narrow hallway into a modern-looking kitchen where a kettle was on the boil. A fresh salad was sitting out on a plate, waiting to be eaten.

'Hello?'

A brown-haired woman walked into the kitchen with eyes so blue they were the brightest thing in the street. A fever of freckles was scattered on her cheeks.

For a moment – just a moment – I thought she was going to topple over. Then she leaped towards her daughter and screamed and cried and laughed and hugged and Frankie and I just didn't know where to look!

'How did you get here? How are you, love?'

'How've you been, Mum?'

'Oh God, it's good to see you, pet!'

A stream of words and phrases buzzed between them. I wanted to get off side but, let's face it, there wasn't much room in that kitchen, and Frank and I weren't about to squeeze past an amorphous weeping lump that was Mother and Daughter.

'I'm great, love. Terrific!' Lauren's mum was saying. 'Just missing you, that's all. So how come you're here?'

'Well, erm, I just wanted to see that you're alright, Mum. I, we, sort of … borrowed a car to get here,' Lauren answered, looking at us two for help.

'Borrowed?' her mum asked.

'Yeah, Mum. I'll explain in a minute, but come on,

tell me all about you. Why didn't you come to visit last week?'

'Oh, I'm sorry, love – I wanted it to be a surprise. I had a job interview. Civil Service. And I got it, love!'

'Mum! That is *fan-tas-tic*! When do you start?'

'Next week. Oh, I'm so nervous, pet. But I'm really looking forward to it. It's a new beginning, Lauren – for both of us.'

Mrs Murray guided her daughter into the front living room, half laughing, half crying. She didn't look like an alcoholic, but then again, what does an alcoholic look like? It's not like they wear a badge or something declaring that they've got an illness. Mrs Murray was smart and pretty and the front room was tidier than ours at home. There were framed photos of Lauren everywhere.

'So are these your friends?' she asked, nodding towards us.

'Yeah, sort of,' Lauren laughed. 'This is Ben from the 'burbs and you remember Frank? He used to live two doors down?'

'Of course! I didn't recognise you at first, Frank. You've really changed – turned into a fine-looking fella.'

Frank Morgan's face blushed the same colour as his hair. Seriously! Mr Hard Man himself was putty in this woman's hands and loving every minute of it.

'You look sort of familiar too, Ben. Did you ever live around here?' she asked.

I swear the hairs stood up on the back of my neck. I felt as if I *had* lived round here, but that was just my stupid imagination.

'No, Mrs Murray. I grew up on Chester Road,' I said. Meekly. What was it about this woman that turned Frankie Boy and me into choir boys?

She was staring at me now, sizing me up.

'Strange,' she said. 'I thought I knew you.'

'Mum, what are you doing with these?' Lauren asked then, rifling through a bunch of travel brochures on the sofa.

'Well, you're always saying how much you want to travel, pet. I thought we could maybe save up and go somewhere nice. Italy, France, anywhere.'

Mrs Murray's smile was as wide as her daughter's and for a minute or two Frankie and I felt real awkward sitting plonk in the middle of this happy family reunion.

Lauren was throwing her arms around her mum and talking about the Mediterranean, the Adriatic, and I'm not sure where else when suddenly there was a furious knocking at the door.

'Who on earth's banging at the door? Ach no,

Lauren – are you in some kind of trouble?'

Mrs Murray looked really worried now. She glanced at each of us and then answered the door.

Ten seconds later Allie Cooper and Chris the Priss walked in, and they were not happy!

'*Of all the stupid, dumb, brainless things to do!*' hissed Allie. '*What the hell were you all thinking of?*'

I'd never seen Allie mad before, and it wasn't a pretty sight! She was fuming!

'Driving a car without experience? Without a license? You could have been killed!'

Technically, Frankie wasn't without experience, but I didn't feel the need to point that out at this particular moment.

'Don't you know this will go on your record?' she was saying now. 'Have you no idea how to actually behave like *normal* teenagers?'

What the hell were *they*? Again, I didn't put this question forward either.

'I had to see Mum, Allie,' Lauren said. 'I know it was stupid – dead stupid – but I was just so worried about her!'

Lauren's mum was shaking her head, tears springing from her eyes. Not understanding what was going on.

'Don't you think I'd have told you if your mum needed help, Lauren?' Allie asked. 'Don't you realise I've been keeping an eye on her? I know how worried you've been and I would never have let anything happen to your mum!'

'You have? But … but, I didn't know that, Allie, I didn't know,' Lauren sobbed.

Allie fell into a chair and buried her face in her hands.

'You kids!' she said. 'You have no idea! No idea how much the staff at Knockmore do for you. We're in contact with your families all the time! We don't always put you in the picture because you need space to heal. You three are so busy, running around feeling sorry for yourselves, that you can't see what's right in front of you!'

'And, ahem, there's the small matter of my car,' interrupted Chris.

'Not now, Chris. We'll deal with that later, love,' said Allie.

Love? Yuck!

'Is Lauren in big trouble, Allie?' Mrs Murray asked. 'It's all my fault! If I was a fit mother she wouldn't have to act like this.'

Allie's face seemed to soften.

'You *are* a fit mother, Kerry!' she said, taking Mrs Murray's hand. 'You've been through such a lot in life it's hardly surprising that you break from time to time. I know you've never got over what happened to Lauren's dad.'

'But I'm weak, Allie. Look at you – losing your sister in that accident. You don't hit the bottle like I do!'

'I've had my own demons, Kerry, you know that. Knockmore is my refuge – as much as it is for the kids. And anyway, things are on the up for you what with your new job and everything. We just need Lauren here to stay out of *borrowed* cars and we'll be sorted.'

There was a glimmer of a smile from Allie now, but I could see that Chris the Priss was straining to look at his precious car through the window. Unfortunately, there wasn't as much as a dent on it. Just my regurgitated breakfast.

'Now, time to get everybody back. Chris will drive his car and take Ben with him, and you two will come with me. Lauren, say goodbye to your mum. Frank, if you'd like to, we can stop off at old Joe's house on the way back. Just for some memories. And Ben – *behave!*'

Lauren hugged her mum and Allie promised Mrs Murray that her daughter wouldn't get into trouble.

And with that we were briskly removed from 42 Simon Street, but not before Mrs Murray took my hand and looked at me with an odd expression.

'Goodbye, Ben,' she said. 'Come back again.'

I nodded. I knew I probably would.

Mrs Murray stood at her front door, obviously intending to wave her daughter off, but Allie and Chris ushered all three of us down to where they had parked Allie's car and Mrs Murray took the hint and retreated inside, closing her door.

Allie and Chris put their heads together and muttered for a few moments, then Allie turned to us.

'Guys, it's time to be straight with each other,' she said. 'I know you think there's something funny going on back at Knockmore, and you're right. But we'll talk about that later. Right now you need to know that we have your best interests at heart. Ben – Chris visits your family regularly. Frank, Jack keeps your foster parents informed. Lauren, I visit your mum – because I knew Helen Crawford couldn't.'

She said this last bit out of the corner of her mouth, but to be honest I was still hung up on the image of Chris the Priss visiting *my* home. God knows what he'd been telling them! And what *was* going on at Knockmore?

Chapter twenty-two

'We're paying a visit to your house on the way, Ben,' Chris said with a sly smile. 'I'm sure your folks will be delighted with your latest act of lunacy!'

'Don't think you're actually supposed to call me a lunatic, Chris. Haven't you got a code of conduct or something you're supposed to follow?'

God, I hated this guy! He must break every rule in the staff-resident handbook!

'Oh, but Ben, I am committed to helping you adopt positive, proactive behaviour. It's my whole purpose in life,' he sneered.

'Yeah, right!'

'Seriously, Ben, you really need to stop thinking the world's against you. You and your mates steal *my* car – *and* you vomit all over it for good measure – but you expect me to say 'No problem'? You gotta start taking a bit of responsibility for the things you do, mate, and stop behaving like the world owes you a favour.'

I rolled my eyes in what I hoped was an aggressive way, but it probably just ended up making me look like a tosser.

'Your mum and dad are good guys, you know. Maybe you should give them a break.'

He had this annoying habit of speaking like an Aussie with the end of every sentence sounding like a question. He thought he was the coolest dude this side of the Western Hemisphere! The Chris.i.am of Belfast City!

We pulled up and I swear I nearly choked. It had only been a few weeks but, boy, had I missed this place! Without even realising it.

Mum was weeding in the front garden and Gran was watching her from a deckchair. Amy was up a tree. No change there then. Probably looking for creepy crawlies to adopt.

Mum's cry of 'Ben! Oh son, it's so good to see you!' was followed almost instantly by 'What has he done?' in a deadpan voice.

'We'll go into that later, Mrs Parker,' Chris the Priss said smoothly. 'For now, it's just a social call.'

God, he was a smarmer when he wanted to be, smiling at my mum with his Colgate smile. He even removed his ever-present baseball cap to speak to her. *Yuck!* This prat was seriously flirting with my mother! No wonder he called out to the house so often.

'Ben, you look so – healthy!' Gran said, pulling herself up. 'The fresh air obviously suits you out there at Knockmore. And you've beefed up too. A proper young man,' she said, cuddling me like I was anything but.

'You look good too, Gran,' I said, taking in the newly cut hair and frozen face. She'd obviously paid another visit to Holywood lately, County Down's capital of plastic surgery.

'*Ben!*' yelled Amy from the tree.

'Hi, Ames!' I shouted up to where she was wriggling around like a koala. 'Find anything disgusting up there?'

She jumped out of the tree like a squirrel on Red Bull.

'What are you doing here, Ben? Are you finished being bad?'

'Not just yet, Amy. But I will be soon.'

I'm sure I heard a snort from my baseball-hat-less buddy beside me but I let it go.

'Just here for a visit.'

'So they're looking after you, son?' Gran said. 'Feeding you plenty of protein?' And then her face changed suddenly. 'They're not making you dig tunnels or anything, are they, love?'

'No, Gran, no tunnels. Just lots and lots of therapy crap.'

'Oh, therapy's good, Ben. Gets rid of one or two demons. Doesn't do much for the wrinkles though ...' Her voice faded out as she moved her deckchair into the shade.

Mum was carrying a tray of cold drinks out from the kitchen.

'From what Chris tells me, you're really adjusting to life at Knockmore,' she said. 'He says you're really good with the horses.'

He did?

'Er, yeah, Mum, they're sort of cool,' I muttered. 'Especially Sky.'

'Is she the big grey mare I've been hearing about?' she asked, handing me a can of Coke.

Crikey – so they really *were* kept informed! What else did they know?

'I told you years ago to take up horse-riding,' she said, readjusting her sunglasses. 'But young boys – they just don't listen to their mothers, do they?' She laughed – a weird operatic laugh that seemed to be for the benefit of Chris.

I let the ice-cold Coke fizz like a firework down my throat and decided to ignore what could only be described as middle-aged flirting. And, unlike my usual self, I concentrated on the good things – the sharp summer smell of freshly cut grass, the sun shining, and most of all, being at *home*.

'Ben!' Ames said. 'Come and see my new tarantula. It's orange and black and I've called it Talula.'

'Of course you have! What else would you call a tarantula?'

All remains of Sindy's short life had been removed from the landing *and* from Amy's affections, by the look of it. She had new friends now – the tarantula, a gecko, a pair of stick insects and what looked like a box turtle.

'So, when *are* you coming home?' she asked after I admired them all.

'Soon, Ames. Soon. When I get to the bottom of things.'

'The bottom of what? You belong here, Ben, not on some funny-farm.'

Very politically correct, my wee sister.

'I just need to suss some things out, Ames. Then I'll be done.'

'You mean your real i-dent-y?' she said, giving 'identity' three syllables.

'Yeah, that. But, you know, I sort of need time out for a while too. I miss being home. I miss you, Ames. But I sort of hope that by the time I come back for good – well, I'll be *better*. Do you know what I mean?'

'Sort of,' she said, putting the tarantula back in its case. 'Does it mean you won't row with Mum and Dad all the time?'

'Not sure that I can promise that, Amy, but maybe I can cut the rows down to – I dunno, five a day?'

''Kay,' she said. 'But it's a bit boring without you, Ben.'

'What? Even with all your reptile friends?'

She was doing that thing where she twiddles her hair around until it's wrapped so tightly round her finger it gets stuck, and then she screams like a cat caught in a cement-mixer.

'Look, Amy, I'll be home in a few weeks and we can play hide-and-go-seek and jump on the trampoline until midnight. Just hang on in there, okay?'

'I will,' she said. 'But, Ben, can you make it a bit quicker cos Dad's, like, in a really bad mood without you.'

'Dad? You sure about that? Probably just dreading me coming back home.'

'Nah, it's not that,' she said, shaking her head.

'He misses having a *boy* around. I heard him telling Mum. Said the place is way too quiet without you.'

Mmm. Dad, missing *me*? I'd have to have a think about that one.

I gave Amy a cuddle. Not a manly, detached sort of cuddle but a proper tight squidgy squeeze. Then I went back to the garden where Mum was still grinning like a Cheshire Cat.

'Oh, Ben, I'm so glad you've benefited from Knockmore. Chris is telling me about all the progress you've made. We can't wait to have you home!'

I eyeballed Chris who was nodding his head and stroking his beard like some kind of guru.

'Yes, Mrs Parker – he's come a long way. We're very proud of him at the centre. He's much less emotionally reactive than when he first arrived.'

Emotionally what? God, he was such a liar! Or maybe he wasn't – maybe I actually was making progress and Chris wasn't the Devil's Spawn after all?

'But we'll have to go now,' he said. 'This was just a flying visit. We've one or two little matters to sort out back at the farm.' And he put his arm around me like we were bezzies.

'Bye, darling!' said Gran. 'Make sure you take plenty of protein shakes. You'll want to keep that nice butch look you've got now. It's very becoming.'

'Yes, Gran,' I replied, raising my eyes to the highest heaven and giving her a hug.

I hugged Mum and Ames and then Chris ushered me back to the car.

'How come you didn't tell Mum the truth?' I asked Chris when we had set off.

'I did. You *have* come a long way. You're not quite the nasty, arrogant little plonker you were at the beginning.'

'Cheers, Chris,' I said. 'I think.'

'Besides, I didn't want to worry your mum. She's been real anxious about you so I reckoned she didn't need any more aggro.'

'Do you fancy my mum or something?'

'Trust you to say something like that, Ben. I have no interest whatsoever in your mum – other than a professional one. She just needs a break, that's all.'

That much I knew. Mum had had this dream growing up that she was going to save the world – fix everyone's problems. Dad said she was an idealist and that was one of the reasons why he fancied her. 'That and the sun-kissed hair!' They met in Belfast when they were both at Queen's University and he said she was just so bright and breezy and full of sun. Which is amazing considering all the crap with the 'Troubles' was going on then.

Poor Mum. She had tried so hard in vain to fix *me*.

'And anyway, there's no need for *anyone* else to know about the little joyriding "episode",' Chris said, interrupting my thoughts.

'There isn't?' I asked. Confused.

'No, Ben. We'll let it drop … for now.'

'We will?'

'Yes, Ben. In return for …'

Ah, here it was – the blackmail I was waiting for.

'In return for what?' I asked.

'In return for you telling Allie and me what you learned when you hacked into John Wilson's computer.'

'*You know about that?*' I squealed. Well, sort of shrieked.

'I know about everything, Ben' he said, touching his nose like he was bloody Wolverine!

'Well, if you know *everything*, why do you need me to tell you more?' I said, proud of my pedantics.

'Yin and Yang, Ben. A little give and take. Allie and I are worried about Knockmore, and we think you can help us. But obviously that's up to you. No-one's going to force you.'

This plonker was such a cliché! But, then again, maybe he did want to help the centre. And maybe *I* did too.

Chapter twenty-three

'So, what do you want to know?' I asked.

Frank, Lauren, Heath and I had been called into the Nendrum Room by Chris and Allie. We hadn't told Heath anything about borrowing Chris's car because Allie said it would really knock him back.

We were sitting in a circle, ready to share the *Secrets of Knockmore*, when the Honcho stuck his head round the door.

'Mini-meeting, Chris?'

'That's right, John. Just a select few tonight for some intensive therapeutic intervention,' said Chris.

Sounded painful to me, but I did my best to mirror the Colgate smile and nod my head.

'Okay then. Carry on!' the Honcho said.

And off he went, none the wiser, as my gran would say.

I could see Allie letting out the breath she'd been holding in.

'So, what is going on around here?' I asked.

'First of all, tell us what *you* know!' Chris the Priss hissed (actually, that's quite hard to say out loud).

'*Okaaay* ... Keep your hair on!' I said, savouring the moment. 'Knowledge is power,' my history teacher used to say. And he was right.

'So, Knockmore is undersubscribed,' I went on. 'And there's some connection with Helen Crawford, but I haven't figured that one out yet.'

'I have,' interrupted Allie, raking her fingers through her hair. 'She's supplying the clients in order to keep Knockmore afloat. I just haven't worked out why.'

'She's trying to save this place?' I asked. 'By packing it full of eejits like us?'

'Your words, not mine, Ben. But yes, it looks that way. She seems to have given each of you a reason to come here.'

'But it's costing my mum and dad a bloody fortune!' I said. 'How is everybody else affording it?'

'Oh, rub it in, rich boy! We're not scobes, you know!' Lauren's voice. Like scissors.

'Helen Crawford somehow manages to get the local Young People's Trust to part-fund it,' Allie explained. 'The council was our biggest funder but they've had to cut their contribution. Recession, of course. The thing is, I'm pretty sure John Wilson knows what she's up to. In fact, he actively supports it, by the looks of it.'

'He must be crappin' himself that it's going to be closed down and he's gonna drown in debts!' said Frank. 'He'll have to sell the house and farm for sure!'

'To be fair,' Chris interrupted, 'I think he really believed in this place. Once. Now he's just up to his neck in debts and he's thrashing around looking for options.'

Allie gave him a weird, googly-eyed look that sort of made my stomach heave. There's just no accounting for taste! Chris took his baseball cap off and grinned back at her.

'But it's bound to be illegal,' I said. 'Isn't it? Signing people in here for half-baked reasons?'

'Probably,' Allie nodded. 'But then again, you all wanted to come here – for different reasons. Maybe Helen was just giving you the nudge you needed?'

'But she can't keep "nudging" saddos to come here! She's bound to run out of "troubled teens" at some point,' Lauren said. Arms folded.

'True. I think it's just a sticking plaster at the

minute,' said Allie. 'I don't know what John's going to do in the long term.'

I still couldn't figure out why we'd all been evacuated to Nendrum the day before. What was he up to when we were all learning about ancient bloody monks at Nendrum?

'John had the place valued when we were all off site,' Allie explained as if she'd read my thoughts. 'Seems there's a big buyer interested.'

'That's good. Isn't it? Won't the place still run then?' Lauren asked. Doubtfully.

'Not as a healing centre,' Allie answered. 'But as a five-star golf resort.'

'*Whaaat?* We've more golf courses around here than you can shake a stick at. What do we want another one for?' I squeaked. 'I mean – *seriously*? Who does he think he is? Donald-bloody-Trump?'

'Apparently international tourists are what's needed for Northern Ireland's future – not our own homegrown next generation. Welcome to the world of money-making and self-interest.' Allie was shaking her head. And I was pretty sure those song-thrush eyes had tears in them.

'But do you reckon Helen Crawford was lying to us all to encourage us to come here?' I asked. 'I mean, was she lying to us about … what we'd find here?'

I lifted my head and squinted. Hoping.

'The truth is, Ben – I don't know.' said Allie. 'Helen doesn't always follow the accepted path, but I do think that she's sincere, if misguided. I honestly don't know what she told each of you – but I do know that she's got a heart in there. Somewhere.'

I noticed her looking at Chris. Waiting for his reassurance.

'My mum knew Helen – I mean, my adoptive mum,' I said, as if that really needed explaining at this point. 'I think Helen screwed up a bit at work. Kind of cut corners, that sort of thing.'

'She was very keen to get me in here,' said Lauren stiffly, with a hard jaw. 'Told me I needed time out. Needed to be a teenager again.'

'Well, she wasn't wrong, Lauren – I can't disagree with that,' Allie nodded. 'You do have to learn to look out for yourself.'

'But I *can* look out for myself, Allie! I just love being with Mum. Why can't anyone get that? She's my best friend!'

Allie went over to her and hugged her. Tight. 'I know, love. I know. Mums are important,' she said. 'Very important.'

Erm, hello? Heath was in the room, Frank was in the room, *I* was in the room! A little more sensitivity, please!

As if on cue, Allie looked at each one of us.

'I know you all feel lost. Each one of you. But you're not, that's what I've been trying to make you see. Frank – your foster parents want you to stay with them for as long as you want. Ben, your mum and dad and little sister are lovely. Appreciate them, *please*! And Heath – I know there's very little I can say, except that you've got me. You've always had me!'

And then it came. The information that left us all stunned.

'I'm sorry I couldn't be a mother to you, Heath – instead of just an aunt,' Allie was saying. 'But when your mum and dad died – well, I fell apart too. But I never left you. You know that. You went to a good home and I always, *always* looked out for you.'

I could hear breathing. And a clock. And noises in the dark outside. But I couldn't move. No-one could.

Until:

'I know that, Auntie Allie,' said Heath quietly. 'And I know you bring me here so we can be together at this time of year. But I just wish someone would tell me the truth. The whole truth, and nothing but the truth!'

His bluntness had real power. It made people gasp for air and drop their jaws. I know that's what each of us did in the Nendrum Room that night.

'Bloody hell!' said Frank.

Yep. My thoughts exactly. Heath and Allie were related? And why was it a big secret up until now? I looked from one to the other and realised that they looked quite alike. Allie's eyes really were brimming over now. For Heath, for Knockmore – for the place where they could be together. So Heath's mum was Allie's sister – the same sister who had died in a car accident? Jesus! I did kind of wonder why she hadn't taken Heath in herself, all those years ago. But hey – who was I to judge? Allie had talked about her 'demons' before, at Lauren's mum's house. Maybe she was just too broken back then. Seemed like we all carried baggage around in here – even the counsellors. Maybe that was why they understood so much.

Chapter twenty-four

'Ben? Are you awake?'

Of course I was awake. How could anybody sleep after a revelation like that?

'Yeah, why?' I whispered back.

'Can I come in?'

Oh boy! Luscious Lauren was asking if she could come into my bedroom in the middle of the night and I couldn't even answer her! Shell shock. Or something.

'Ben?'

'Yeah, yeah – come in!' I muttered. Eventually.

I fumbled around with the duvet and tried to cover myself up. I felt like an oven-ready chicken smothered in tinfoil, peeping out at her from behind my bedclothes.

'Er, hello,' I said. 'Haven't seen you here before.'
Pathetic.

'Ben, I can't believe it,' she said, sitting down in her PJs on the edge of my bed. 'I cannot believe what we heard tonight! I thought I knew Allie, but she's never breathed a word of this, not a word!'

I could hardly breathe.

'Yeah, it's a – it's a revelation, alright,' I nodded. Sagely.

'She and her family left Simon Street before I was born,' she said. 'I had no idea that she had lost her sister like that.'

'Guess we all have our secrets,' I said. 'But this place has a way of making them come out.'

'I had never even heard Heath *speak* before!' said Lauren, squishing herself up closer to me on the bed.

'I did. Once,' I said, pulling my knees up to my chest in case some part of me actually touched her. 'We talked about horses.'

'He spoke to *you*? Really, Ben? About *horses*?'

'Yeah, *really*, Lauren. Why does that shock you so much? I'm not the friggin' devil incarnate, you know!'

'I know, I know,' she said. 'But that means he must have felt kinda close to you. That's so cool.'

'It is?'

'Yeah. He must have seen something in you that made him want to relate to you.'

Uh-oh! She'd gone all Knockmore on me.

'Don't know about that,' I muttered. 'He just speaks when he feels like it, and I happened to be the one that was around.'

'What's this? Ben Parker being modest?' she laughed. 'Take the credit when it's due, Ben. He obviously felt comfortable with you and that's really nice.'

She was inching towards me again. I could smell her shampoo. My lips felt dry. Heath might have felt comfortable, but right at this moment I was anything but! Don't get me wrong – I'm not allergic to girls or anything. I'm just *cautious*. Especially when I'm in this place on a mission. And the mission doesn't involve falling head over heels in love with one of the inmates!

'What do you think Heath meant when he said he wanted the truth?' she asked.

'Dunno. Guess he just wants to know more about what happened to his parents. Maybe Allie hasn't talked much about the car accident to him.'

She nodded her head. Thinking. Then she pushed right up beside me and laid her head on the pillow.

'Give us a hug, Ben. Apart from Allie, no-one hugs in here. I miss my mum's cuddles.'

'Uh, okay,' I said. Expressive as always.

She lifted the duvet and curled into me and I could almost taste the chewing gum on her breath. All minty and fresh. Her hair was sort of tickling my chin but I was damned if I was going to move it out of the way. I was frozen to the spot! I could feel her hear beating against my chest and my whole body surged.

'So, did you like my mum, Ben? She's pretty cool, isn't she?'

'Yeah, er, yeah, she is, I suppose,' I answered, barely breathing.

'She liked *you*,' she said. 'Dunno why.' That high laugh again. 'She thought she recognised you from somewhere. I told her she couldn't have. You've probably just got one of those faces.'

'What? Are you saying I'm *common* or something? Like, just an everyday run-of-the-mill Joe Friggin' Soap? Gee, thanks, Lauren. And there was me thinking I was someone a bit special.'

I was joking obviously. You know, being *ironic*. But Lauren looked at me all seriously as if she'd bruised me in the face or something.

'You *are* a bit special, Ben. You just don't know it.'

And then it came. Warm, spongy lips against mine. I had never been kissed before. I mean *never*! And here it was, the gorgeousist girl in Belfast moving her mouth against mine and the things that were happening to me at that moment CANNOT be described. Unless you've been there. Holy shit! This was way better than, than – I dunno! Better than anything!

'I've been wanting to kiss you since you arrived,' she said, in between snogging me. 'But I didn't know it would be this good!'

I was good? *Yeeessss!!* I could feel her breath warm on my face and I could feel judders up and down my flesh and it was, like, OUT OF THIS WORLD! I was seriously going to explode.

And then:

'What the *hell* is going on here?'

Jack the Lad. Spoiling the BEST MOMENT IN MY LIFE!

'*Lauren, what are you doing in here?*' he shrieked. '*Back to your own room – now!*'

He had a face like a wet weekend in Warrenpoint.

'What are you up to, Parker? I knew I couldn't trust you. *Knew* it!' His face was screwing up with a mixture of fury and excitement.

Lauren ran past him but he was too busy venting his fury on me to even notice her.

'Wait till John Wilson hears this. You'll be out of here on your ear, Parker!'

'I–I–I–' was all I could say. An MLA in the making.

'What the hell did you think you were doing – luring that wee girl in here?'

'I–I–I–' Yep, there I went again.

'Horny wee –! You'll get your comeuppance – I'll see to that!'

I didn't hear the next bit. He was off down the corridor like a sergeant major high on Joose, searching for the first person he could tell his wee dirty story to. I didn't care. I'd experienced Nirvana – whatever that was – and I was never going back to Ben the Unkissed. For the rest of my life I would know that I'd been kissed by Lauren Murray. With her silky dark hair and her blue eyes and her pink stone thing around her neck. And it was absolutely bloody brilliant!

Chapter twenty-five

I couldn't sleep. It wasn't just the thought of Lauren, it was the crushing heat. Hard to believe, but Norn Iron was actually having *another* heat wave! Two heat waves in one month – a second searing, creaking heat that we hadn't seen in who knows how long? Sweat itched between my legs and the duvet felt like an electric blanket. I kicked like a farting foal all night.

'Time to get up!' Jack the Lad was shouting.

He just couldn't wait for me to get my comeuppance – or some such word he had yelled last night. Great! Judgement Day had come. I threw on a T-shirt and a pair of shorts and made my way down to the breakfast room.

Lauren was there, looking sheepish with a slice of toast. Heath was staring into the distance. And Frank – well, Frank was pushing two fried eggs into his mouth.

'Hiya,' I said to Lauren. 'You okay?'

'Yeah, you?'

'So far. Haven't had the inquisition yet.'

'Listen, Ben, I'll tell them the truth,' she said, pushing the toast away. 'I'll tell them I came to your room, that it was all my fault.'

'Nah, it's alright. No point two of us getting in trouble. I'm happy to take the blame,' I said. Very nobly. Feeling six feet tall. I was standing in front of the girl I had snogged the night before *and* I was being her knight in shining armour! Big Guns Ben! I was feeling pretty good.

'Well, at least you're probably going to miss out on the self-comfort skills session today,' she said, laughing. 'Apparently it's to help reduce *impulsivity*.'

I thought again about our impulsivity the night before and wondered why anyone would want to reduce that!

'Ben, can you come here, please?'

It was the Honcho. My time had come.

'Comin', Mr Wilson,' I said, all polite and respectful. Well, it wouldn't hurt, would it?

I followed him to his office and thought – what's

the worst that can happen? I get thrown out of here and have to go home? That wasn't so bad actually – I had become less obsessed with the whole 'Who do you think you are?' thing. And I was sure I'd get to see Lauren and the others again – I mean, they would be out of here soon anyway.

He sat in his leather chair and grinned at me just like he'd done on Day One. He wasn't the type to get straight to the point. I knew I was in for at least half an hour of psychobabble first.

'What do you think you've learned here, Ben?' he said, his hands joined together.

I decided to humour him.

'Erm, I've learned to be less self-centred,' I answered. I thought it was a pretty good answer, but apparently it wasn't enough.

'And what else?'

'Okaay, I … I … miss my family,' I said. Nodding.

I was doing pretty well here, I thought. *And* I was telling the truth. Plus it was nice and cool in his office which was a bit of a relief. The rest of the place felt like one big greenhouse.

He was looking at me steadily now. Good. I waited for the business with Lauren to be brought up but he still wasn't ready to launch his attack. At least that's what I thought.

'But I want to know more, Ben.'

'You do?' Friggin' hell – what else was I supposed to say? 'That's basically it, John – I mean, Mr Wilson.'

'But it isn't, Ben, is it? You've learned other things too!'

Shit! I'd run out of things. Was I supposed to, like, just make things up?

'You've learned all sorts, haven't you, Ben? Right here in my office – when you were hacking into my computer!'

His smile had gone. The joined hands were no longer joined. In fact, he looked pretty bloody cross. And his caterpillar eyebrows seemed to be getting closer and closer to mine across the desk.

'You …you don't want to talk about last night? *With Lauren?*' I squeaked.

'I don't give a bloody damn about last night! I want to know why *my* camera picked you up sitting in *my* chair with your fingers on *my* computer the other night. *That's* what I want to know, Ben! I know Frank Morgan was in here too before, but I'm guessing you were the *brains* behind it all.'

A camera? There was a camera? I looked around wildly but couldn't see one.

'*Oh, okay,*' I squeaked again. If anybody anywhere ever finds a way of putting an end to this friggin' squeak in my voice, I swear I'd give them everything I've got. Which isn't much but … 'Erm, I

was just, you know, trying to look up a few things,'
I said. Unconvincingly.

'Like what?' he thundered.

'Like, like … anything really.' I shrugged, like a
helpless moggy.

Then he was out of his seat, coming round the
table towards me and I jumped out of my seat like
out of a catapult.

'You can't hit me, you know! You can't touch me,
Wilson! It's not allowed! You're a man of calm,
remember? A counsellor? A pacifier?'

I was darting around the room now while he just
followed me round in circles looking like Lucius
Malfoy.

'Seriously, John – I think you need to check your job
description. Slaying one of the kids defo isn't on it!'

'Shut up, you little middle-class twat!' he shouted.
'And tell me what you know!'

Bloody adults – when will they ever learn not to
expect us to shut up *and* speak at the same time? My
English teacher would have said he was using an
oxymoron, but right now the only thing that made
sense in this room was the last bit – *moron!*

'John? What on earth's going on?'

A song thrush. Saving me.

'Allie! Allie, he's mad! He's lost the plot!' I shrieked.

'John?' she asked again. 'Explain!'

'Him! Nosy Parker – *he's* what's wrong! Snooping around trying to find out my business! I won't have it, Allie! He's out on his ear! I won't have this kind of behaviour!'

'So you were going to what? Assault him? Was that your solution?'

I was behind Allie by this stage, cowering like a midget, not a six-foot-tall knight.

'I'll – I'll bloody kill him if I have to!'

I swear he was foaming at the mouth now.

'You're not going to kill anyone, John. You're going to calm down, take a seat and count yourself lucky that I walked in when I did,' she said quietly. 'Otherwise you're going to find yourself locked up somewhere with no air conditioning, no leather chairs and no cool green carpets. Somewhere like Maghaberry Prison for instance.'

He looked frightened now. Really unnerved. Shifting from one foot to the other. Then he sat down as he was told and cried like a baby.

'I don't know what to do, Allie. I just don't know what to do.'

'You start by telling us what's going on. And you follow that up with not battering the kids.'

His head sank into his hands. He was muttering apologies over and over again until I actually started to feel sorry for the bloke. His comb-over was matted with sweat.

'Ben, go and get Chris, will you?' said Allie, walking towards Wilson like he was a wild horse needing taming.

By the time I got back she was kneeling beside him, speaking slowly, soothing him.

'You should have let the rest of the team know Knockmore was in trouble,' she was telling him. 'What you've done is wrong, John, on every level! Getting Helen to scoop up youngsters left, right and centre, to try and keep the place open? What were you thinking? And what's in it for her anyway?'

'She's my sister-in-law,' he wept. 'She was just trying to keep the place afloat.'

Allie raised her eyes to Chris who was watching it all from the doorway, with Frank, Lauren and Heath in tow.

'You do realise Helen will never work again after this. She's already been struck off in Social Services. And you, John – you *know* I'm going to have to report what I saw here today.'

'Today is the least of my worries, Allie,' he blubbered. 'It gets worse. Much worse.'

Jesus, what else had he done? Buried a body? Done a deal with the Dissidents? Run around naked at Nendrum?

'The deal's off with Waters and Waters. They've

pulled out. There's no money – no money at all!'

'And you expect me to be sympathetic? You were going to sell up and you expect me to be sorry that it's fallen through?'

I could tell that Allie was doing her best to keep calm, but her voice had a tremor in it that sounded like it might turn into an eruption.

'I'm ruined, Allie. Ruined. What am I going to do?' he sobbed.

And I suddenly really felt I wanted to put things right. We all did. Knockmore was a harbour, a refuge, and though we might all be as mad as a box of frogs, it would be terrible to lose it.

'Kids,' said Allie, blowing her fringe, 'you really shouldn't be hearing any of this but, the fact is, you're here and you know the facts. What can we do?'

Allie was asking *us* for help? We were in a seriously bad way!

'Get donations,' said Frankie. 'Something like that.'

'Sounds easy – but how?' Allie asked, clearly taking Frankie seriously.

'I dunno. Some kind of fundraising. Haven't really figured it out yet. But I will,' he said, scratching his head.

Uh-oh, this was going to be a long day. Frank in full cerebral mode was a scary sight. Dandruff would be flying everywhere!

'It would have to be an awful lot of fundraising to keep this place afloat,' Chris sneered.

Allie nodded at him like he was some kind of spiritual leader with all the answers. They were deluded – the lot of them. Fundraising? What were they expecting? To raise millions at a bun sale? Cadge cash at a car-boot sale? This place was doomed and that was all there was to it.

'Right, let's get out of here, kids,' said Allie. 'We'll leave John to mewl in peace.'

She flung a disgusted look at the Honcho and ushered us all out.

'Not a word to anybody else, guys – you hear?' she said.

'We hear,' Lauren answered. 'But there's an awful lot of weirdness going on around this place.'

'Trust me,' said Allie, putting a hand on her shoulder. 'John is … well, he isn't well at the minute. The stress of trying to save this place has, shall we say, affected him. But we'll get help for him – get him to see a doctor – and sort the rest of it out somehow.'

Lauren was right. None of us had signed up for all this *crap*. Maybe we should all just get out of here and let Knockmore fall like a house of cards.

My guts hurt. And when I looked over to Heath he had disappeared. He didn't deserve any of this.

Chapter twenty-six

And worse was to come.

After the others left I kept looking for Heath. And that was how I ended up down at Old Miller's cottage when the Honcho came storming along, talking to Helen Crawford on his phone.

I slipped into the old house, crouched down and listened.

'No, no, Helen, I've tried everything – you know I have,' babbled the Honcho as he came to a halt by the cottage wall. 'A fire. It's the only way, Helen – claim on the insurance. Start all over again.'

Whaaat?

Helen must have been arguing against it because Wilson kept mumbling about debts and deficits and how it was the only way.

I'd heard enough. Waiting until his back was turned as he paced up and down, I snuck out of the cottage and moved away as quickly and as quietly as I could.

Any respect I'd ever had for this man (i.e. slightly more than zero) was now gone. He was one big mess and he was going to bring Knockmore down with him. It seriously needed to be rid of John Wilson and his mad management techniques. And greasy comb-over.

'Excuse me?' said Allie, blinking at me. 'Arson? Is he *out of his mind*?' Veins seemed to knot under her skin. Like rope. 'What the hell is he dragging us into? Looks to me like he's trying to land the whole bloody lot of us in prison – or worse, in a grave! Has he lost every brain cell he ever had?'

Frankie, Lauren and I stood silent. This was big. And bad. And really screwed up! The Honcho made us inmates look like Charlie's Angels. After about five minutes of dropped jaws and furrowed foreheads, Frank asked the question we all had in our heads.

'Is he, like, planning to burn us all to death?'

'No!' said Allie. 'No! Of course not! He wouldn't do that! Jesus, what am I thinking? He may have said it but he would never do it!'

'Flippin' hell,' said Lauren. 'We're supposed to come in here to heal, not to be burned to a crisp!'

'No, no – that's never going to happen, Lauren,' said Allie, putting a hand on her shoulder. 'Saying something crazy in a desperate moment is a million miles away from actually doing it! John would never do anything criminal. And he'd never hurt any of you.'

You wanna bet? I was thinking. I watched Allie blow her choppy fringe away for the hundredth time and wondered how she'd forgotten about the Honcho's attempted assault on me less than twenty minutes ago.

Chapter twenty-seven

Midges. All over the place! I battered at them with my hands, trying to get the bloody things away from my arms, my face. Tonight I'd be scratching like Frankie, tearing the skin off my elbows till they bled. I was heading back towards Miller's. Why? I don't know. Looking for some sort of answer maybe. Some kind of solution to our *latest* problem at Knockmore. So much for a therapeutic learning environment!

'*Wait up!*'

Frankie was behind me. And Lauren. The Three-bloody-Musketeers. We were a joke – the whole friggin' lot of us.

'*What do you want?*' I shouted back.

'We're coming with you. We need to think up

some ways of coming up with the dosh.'

'Yeah, right! Like a few quid in your piggy bank is going to put the world to rights.'

I was in a foul mood. All this cheating. This heat. This fakeness. I hadn't expected Knockmore to fix me like a bloody Coldplay song, but all this stuff going on? This was melting me. Bad pun intended.

'Yeah, but I'll think of something,' Frank said, his eyes shining with his new project. 'I might know some people who can find cash, if you know what I mean.'

Jesus! King of the Underworld!

'No, Frank, I don't know what you mean, and you know what? I really don't want to.'

We reached the old cottage and I could feel the evening sun burning my skin. It didn't stop Frankie Boy running around topless though and turning tomato-red. I could see my old mate Jordan and her cow-gang slashing their tails at flies in the distance, and I could feel the pulse of a headache coming on – the sort that comes with thunder. Mum always said that nature has its way of getting ready for storms. Probably the wind would pick up soon and the sky would start to look strange.

'Is this it?' asked Lauren. 'Old Miller's place?'

'Yep, this is it. No roof now but it used to be a cosy wee place,' Frank explained. 'Joe used to come here for fresh mackerel and Matt Miller would fry them up in butter. Friggin' gorgeous!'

'Maybe you could fry some up for bingo prizes? That could save the day,' I smirked.

And then he did it again – lunged at me like a wild coyote. Did we have to have a flippin' fight every time we came to this cottage?

'*Jesus, Frankie – it was only a joke!*' I shouted, trying to dodge his fists.

'*You don't joke about fish. Or Joe. Got it?*' he yelled, grabbing me by the scruff of the neck.

'Got it. Loud and clear, Frankie!'

'Will you two stop messing about?' Lauren said. 'We're here to see if we can come up with solutions! Not practise for WWE!'

Frankie released me and I did my best to breathe. You couldn't take small things like your next breath for granted when you were around Frankie 'The Warrior' Morgan!

'Right. How serious do you think old Wilson was about frying the place?' I panted.

'I dunno,' Frank answered.

'How would he do it?' I wondered, imagining the Honcho setting fire to the curtains. 'It would have to be something fast and furious – he'd have to make a big blaze. No good setting a small fire that could be easily put out.'

'Petrol,' said Frankie. 'Petrol is the way to go.' As

if he'd set fires every day of the week in his past life. Maybe he had.

'But there'd be an investigation and the insurance wouldn't pay if he was found out – which he would be. Who else has a motive? We're all witnesses to the fact *he* has one.'

'Bennie Boy,' said Frankie, hands on hips, 'he's outta his friggin' mind. He wouldn't think of any of that.'

He had a point, for once.

'And, besides, he'd blame it on us, wouldn't he?' Frankie was on top of his game, right enough. 'Troubled teens, huh? I bet that was the plan.'

'Arson was probably just a desperate thought, like Allie said.' Lauren was watching birds skim the surface of the lough. 'He wouldn't actually do it, I'm sure.'

I wasn't sure. I was remembering the babbling mess the Honcho had been, green snot pouring. Outta his friggin' mind, as Frankie put it.

'If he's going to use a lot of petrol, he'd have to stash it somewhere. But not at the house.' Frankie's mind – such as it was – was working.

'Yep. Somewhere not too far from the driveway then?'

Frankie laughed and pointed out at the lough. 'You're forgetting, Bennie Boy. It doesn't have to be brought in by road.'

Then he swung around to face me and clutched at his head with both hands. 'Thunderstruck' was the right word for how he looked.

'What is it, Frankie?' I asked.

His eyes bulged. 'I've seen him down here a lot lately.'

'Who?'

'Wilson.'

'Here? At the cottage?'

'Nah, Ben – at the Amazon Rainforest. Yeah, here at the friggin' cottage! You saw him yourself down here!'

'But what would he be doing down here? When I saw him he was just making a phone call.'

'Maybe he just chills out here,' Lauren offered, shrugging her shoulders.

'Hiding something!' Frank blurted out. And he started darting around the place like Henrietta the Hen.

Then he stopped dead and pointed.

'Look over there!'

'What now?'

'That section of wall – something's different about it. It's kinda bulging.'

'Oh, come on, Frankie – I think we're past the age of looking for secret bloody passageways!' I scoffed.

'I know this house,' Frankie snarled. 'Someone's

been meddling with that bit of the wall. Don't you see?'

Broken waves fizzed below us, slopping against the banks below. I was actually starting to feel seasick again.

'It's sort of hollow,' Frankie said, peering through gaps in the stones.

He was feeling all around it, probably waiting for some secret doorway to open up. All we needed now was that wee biddy, Miss Marple, to pop out.

Something about this whole sorry mystery had given Lauren her spark back. She jumped up and looked through the gap between the stones.

'He's right!' she said.

Frankie pulled her back and then pulled one large loose stone out of the wall.

Lauren bounced forward again. *'Holy Mary Mother of God! There's, like, a wee room in there!'* she screeched.

Well, it wasn't a room. More like a large hole. But, the thing was, there were big jerrycans of oil or something in it. Or maybe petrol.

The three of us looked at each other. This thing was real! Wilson was an out-and-out first-class crazy criminal who was prepared to see the place go up in smoke. And there was no way I was hanging around to watch Rome burn.

Chapter twenty-eight

Mum hadn't always lived in Belfast. She grew up near the harbour in Newcastle, and she always said that you could never really leave the sea behind. She said that, even at night, it was never, ever quiet. In calm weather she would hear the water lapping against the quayside, or she'd listen out for the clack of cockles and mussels as the waves rose over the top of them. When I was little I used to think Mum was a bloody mermaid or something, because she seemed to talk about the sea all the time. Me – I friggin' hated it. The sick salty tang, the feeling of being imbalanced. Give me tarmac and firm ground any day of the week. Maybe my real mum was the same? The funny thing was I was starting to care less and less what she was actually like.

From my bedroom in Knockmore you could hear the sea only sometimes. But you could hear all kinds of other things: cattle mooing, sheep bleating, a gate opening, a phone ringing, or Frankie Morgan snoring like a stormtrooper. Sometimes you heard crying, sometimes laughing.

Tonight I heard a tap-tap on my door and expected to see Frank or Lauren (I should be so lucky).

'Ben?'

I opened up.

It was Allie.

'Can I come in?'

She didn't wait for an answer.

'Ben, all this, it's wrong. You kids shouldn't be caught up in any of this. I'm going to ring Social Services in the morning and have you all taken home. This place is going down the pan.'

'Seriously? We can just *go*?'

'Of course you can. This isn't a prison.'

'Can you take that decision though, Allie?'

'Yes, I can. John has left Knockmore – Chris drove him away an hour ago. He's exhausted – he's been under huge pressure, but I hope he'll get the help he needs. And you kids – well, you'll be better off with parents or in care. Proper care. I'll have to get your parents' approval, of course, tomorrow.'

'Did you tell Social Services about – eh – the arson thing?'

She shook her head.

'Are you going to?'

'Might have to. Seems terrible though to destroy a man for a crazy passing thought.'

Uh-oh. I *really* needed to tell her about the jerrycans. But I didn't want to get into it now.

I took a long look at Allie. Who knew when I'd see her again after we left. Truth was, she'd been my friend in here. Probably one day I'd forget things about her – the smaller, paler shapes of things. But never the way she got me. Understood me.

The fact that the Honcho was off the premises and not about to burn the place down was a huge relief. I could get some sleep now at least.

'I've spoken to all the others too,' Allie went on. 'I want to see you all safe in your homes – especially Heath, and Lauren, and Frank . . .' she blew her fringe, 'and you.'

Ah, so I got tagged on at the end. Did that mean I was the least important? Or the most?

'It's been good, you know. Most of it,' I told her. 'The other kids, the horses, the sea.'

'The sea? You don't even like the sea, Ben! I've seen you at Nendrum, remember? Green as an unripe banana.'

215

She smiled one of her tight smiles. Then she looked away.

'It was as hot as this,' I said, remembering that summer at Portrush. 'Hot, white-sun weather, you know what I mean? Me and Mum and Dad were on the beach. There was a picnic rug, I think. And I wanted to run along the sand and all of a sudden there was this sharp pain, like a knife or fire or something, into my heel.'

'What was it?' Allie asked.

'Weaver fish, Dad said. He carried me to the car and took me to Casualty to get the spine out. I screeched the whole way there. And the rest of the night too. No, I don't like the sea.'

I didn't know why I was telling her this. I guess I'd never had much luck with the sea. Or water of any kind. I thought of the time Dad threw me in the swimming pool when I was four but decided not to tell her that.

'I'm the only one in my family who likes the sea,' she said. 'The rest of them are right scaredy cats. My sister even used to freak out at the paddling pool in Bangor. Weird, isn't it – growing up on an island and being terrified of the sea?'

She laughed softly. Started folding my clothes on the end of the bed into neat piles. Pushed my shoes into a line by the wall.

'Guess I'd better go,' she said then. 'Do the rounds. I'm on duty until six o'clock, then Jack takes over.'

'You look sort of tired,' I said, feeling sorry for her. She was losing Knockmore like she'd lost her sister. 'What will you do, Allie – if this place closes?'

Silence. A shrug of the shoulders.

'Don't know, Ben.'

And she left, the door closing quietly behind her.

Cars racing, street lights as orange as fire. People screaming. Amy crying. I tossed and turned until sweat ran down my legs, shouting out, begging for help. My own squealing woke me up. *Jesus!* What was that all about? I was having nightmares like a wee kid. My heart was thudding in my chest like a jackhammer.

There was a light knocking at the door. Again. Tap-tap-tap.

'Come in!'

The door opened.

'You alright?'

It was Heath. Speaking again.

'Yeah, yeah, I think so. Just – you know, bad dreams.'

He nodded his head like he knew *exactly* what I meant. He was standing at the door, self-conscious, awkward.

'Come on in,' I said.

There was a glint of a smile.

He took a few steps inside my room but didn't sit down.

This bedroom of mine was starting to feel like an airport lounge. No visitors for weeks and then two come along at once. Well, almost at once. But Allie had a reason to come. What was Heath's?

'Wanna drink or something?' he offered.

'Nah, I'm okay. I think.'

But I was still shaking, not sure what was real and what wasn't.

'What are you doing up?' I asked.

'I don't sleep much,' he said, looking down. 'Usually take myself off for a walk around this time. Do a bit of ... thinking.'

'In the middle of the night?'

'Why not? Wanna come?'

'Now?'

'Yeah.'

So I did. I got up out of my soft bed to go traipsing round in the dark with Heathcliff and barely a word spoken between us. But there was a new lightness about Heath, I'd noticed that. Like he was expecting some kind of new start. A kind of floor-swept-clean feeling.

Knockmore looked kind of ghostly at night.

Gravel driveways and wall-to-wall glass soon became leafy trees and fields of grass bleached by all the sun we'd had. They looked sort of pale and wan at this time of night. And the sea, as we came closer, looked like bottle-green glass, reflecting two brown-haired boys standing (almost) shoulder to shoulder.

'Do you remember any of it? The crash?' I asked him. I knew I was taking a risk, bringing it all up, but it just seemed like – I don't know, the right time.

'Yes. But I don't want to talk about that. I never talk about that,' he said quietly. He turned to me then with a sort of confused look. 'They used to wait for me to cry, you know – back at the Home. Wanted me to spill it all out. But I didn't. I couldn't. Maybe if I had, they might have told me more about what happened that night.'

'What was it like? Growing up in a children's home?'

He just shrugged. Probably a stupid question anyway. Maybe his silence for all these years was to ward off stupid, pointless questions. Because, let's face it – they weren't going to change anything.

'Spent most of my time just sort of staring into the dark,' he said finally, 'or sleeping. I just used to keep wondering where everyone had gone. How could a whole family vanish?'

What could I say to that? Part of me felt the same,

but it wasn't the time or place to bring up my story.

'And then I got sick,' he went on. 'At least that's what the matron said. I just remember people fizzing in and out of my room all the time, with tablets and funny looks. Telling me to speak. Telling me to get better. But I couldn't, because everything just felt cold all the time, even though they said I was burning up. And my skin – it was so tight – like – like it was choking me. You know what I mean?'

I didn't, but the lump in my throat was getting bigger and bigger as he spoke. I felt like I had a heartbeat in my ears. Heath had had the crappiest life of anyone I had ever known and I realised all of a sudden how much I admired him. And how much I'd miss him.

'Wanna go see Sky tomorrow?" I asked him. Chances were, I'd never see him again and I really wanted us to go to Sky together. Just one last time.

Heath nodded back at me. And smiled a slow smile.

Chapter twenty-nine

'My da used to roll his own fags,' said Frankie the next morning, tucking into what was going to be his second-last breakfast at Knockmore, like it was just any other day. 'He'd roll them on his knee, pat the tobacco into a line and roll it back and forth, back and forth. Then he'd lick the sides, seal it and light up. His face looked different when he smoked. Sort of calmer.'

'It's just a pity he was wrecking his lungs at the same time,' I said, half under my breath.

'I'm not stupid, Bennie Boy. I know fags can bloody kill! That's why I never touch them. But it was the only time my da looked like he wasn't going to thump me.'

He was laughing as he said this last part, but it

was just a cover, like so many things with Frankie Morgan.

'What about your foster parents – what are they like?' I asked him, trying to make up for my smart-ass comment. After talking with Heath, I could now see that sarcasm and tactlessness were – well, just wrong sometimes.

'They're okay. Kinda soft, though. They keep trying to talk things over with me instead of battering me.'

'Isn't that a good thing?'

'Nah, not when you're used to a clout around the head – the message gets in quicker,' he said, pointing to his head so I could figure out the logic. 'They're picking me up tomorrow. I guess they're alright, but way too clean. I have to friggin' take my trainers off at the front door. And have a bloody shower, like, every *day*!'

'Sounds like torture, Frankie.'

'It is!' he insisted. 'If I ever have kids I'm gonna let them take a bath once a year. And walk around the house covered in shit if they want.'

'Jesus, Frank, you're going to be one hell of a parent!' I said.

'He'll be no worse and no better then you, Ben,' Lauren interrupted. Wisely. 'No parent gets it completely right.'

Well, I knew that. Just like I knew no teenager gets it completely right either. After Mum and Dad told me about my adoption I had acted like a real asshole, complaining about this, moaning about that. I brewed my anger into a thick tar like my gran boiled her tea.

'Must have been hard for them,' I said, thinking my thoughts out loud. 'Wondering when and how they were going to tell me. Hoping I'd take it okay but knowing full well that I wouldn't.'

'I don't really get why you're so angry, Ben. I mean – they're *good* parents,' said Lauren, scrunching up her eyebrows, elbows on the table, holding her face in her hands. 'They chose you and gave you a good life.'

'I know that – *now*,' I said. 'And I'm actually looking forward to going home.'

I could smell fresh-cut hay in the field outside and thought I would probably always remember this smell and remember the day I forgave. I don't mean forgave my parents – or my birth parents – but *myself*. I forgave myself for being a loser that someone wanted to get rid of. I was lucky – Mum and Dad had taken me in and given me their best. And that included Amy. Frank and Heath and Lauren had had it way tougher than me and it was time to abandon the 'Feel Sorry for Ben' club.

'It's gonna be a bit weird though, being at home. Away from here,' Lauren said, staring at her untouched food.

I knew she was worried. Worried that her mum might fall off the wagon, worried that it might be all too much for her.

'Allie will look after you – I'm sure she will,' I said. Hoping.

Lauren just shrugged her shoulders.

Who knew what Allie would be doing next? In one day's time this place would be history for all of us – the cattle, the horses, even the bloody chickens. Allie would miss it – we all would. I looked around at the canteen, at Erin Freeman injecting herself for her diabetes at the far end of our table, laughing with Zach Turner who was still telling *the* worst jokes ever to be heard by the human race.

I looked at Jack and Chris talking football, at Allie gazing at all of us, like a protector.

We had told them about the jerrycans and they were understandably stunned. Then, after arguing back and forth, they decided to leave the cans in place until they could show them to the police. And, to keep the matter as discreet as possible, they would wait until all the kids had left the following morning before they called them.

'Ready to see Sky?' I said, nodding over at Heath.

A nod in return.

'Anyone else fancy coming?'

Frank shook his head. I knew he would. Hens were his thing, not horses. But Lauren said no too, which was more of a surprise. Apparently she and Frankie Boy were going to talk Simon Street one last time, which left me right out of the game. She gave me one of her smiles though. Smiles can light distances, Mum used to say, and she was right. I left them to it and walked with Heath down the 'Big Hill' – *An Cnoc Mór*.

Sky was grazing in the long meadow and she looked majestic – like a warrior at peace. I knew to walk to her gently, not just stumble into the field and take her unawares. Her body was steaming like warm straw.

'Hello there, girl. Too hot out here for you?'

Heath and I tried to palm some of the sweat off her body. I couldn't stand the thought that she might be sweltering in the heat.

'Come on, girl, we'll take a walk over there to the shade.'

I couldn't believe it, but she actually followed us to the edge of the field. I stood under a tree and offered her some grass. She lipped it up without even touching my hand.

'What's going to happen to you, eh?' I asked her.

Like she could answer me back. She looked up at me then with her big conker eyes and I could almost see my reflection in them. She slashed her tail around when I stroked her. I would miss this horse, I really would. Then I looked up and saw Allie walking towards us with a saddle and bridle.

'Hi, Ben. Hi, Heath. I was going to cool Sky down and then take her for a bit of a stroll. You want to help me? I did promise after all.'

She *had* promised us a ride before we left Knockmore, but it was hard to get my head round the fact that we were now at that point. The end. Allie spoke to Sky like a flipping horse whisperer, all calm and reassuring. It was hard to believe this horse was once so angry that nobody could get near her. Allie pulled the bridle thing over Sky's ears and put the metal bit in her mouth. Then she threw the big leather saddle over her body and fiddled underneath to fasten it with something called a girth.

'Right – she's ready. Who's going first?'

Heath and I looked at each other. I nodded at him, telling him to give it a go. He'd been around here longer than me so it seemed like it was only right that he rode her first. Allie passed a riding hat over and held out her clasped hands for Heath's foot. He put his weight on her hands and hoisted himself onto Sky. He looked natural up there, straight-backed and sure. He squeezed Sky with his knees and she walked on ahead of us, pulling slightly at the bit but easing out through the gate nonetheless. She looked bloody brilliant!

'Well done, Heath. That's right, keep the reins tight. Heels down in the stirrups.'

Allie and I walked alongside and there was something about the musty smell of the horse that I liked. Her easy movements, the way she swayed slightly as she walked, looked right. Everything about Sky just looked right.

'You okay, Heath?' Allie asked.

He nodded. We just walked alongside him for I don't know how long. Quiet. Contented. A light mist had started to roll in off the lough and it was very peaceful.

But then Frank started yodelling at us from the top of the hill and running down in our direction like a frigging cheetah.

'*Hey, wait up, you lot!*' he was shouting. '*Lauren wants a go too!*'

Lauren didn't get a go – and neither did I, because right at that moment Sky took off into a gallop, probably spooked by Frankie's madness. Heath didn't make a sound – no real change there – he just arched his back and leaned forward like he was born to it. Allie was shouting at him to hold on, not to panic, but Heath didn't look like he was panicking. He looked free. As he got further and further away from us, though, Allie was really getting nervous.

'*Heath, pull your reins in! Try and steer her back to us!*' she screamed.

Sky's hooves kicked up dry earth, drumming across the field. It was like time stood still – well, Frankie did at least. The thud of Sky's hooves echoed like a heartbeat. I realised I was holding my breath. Then eventually Heath moved Sky back towards us and the horse started to slow into a trot and then a walk. I ran towards her and caught her bridle. Heath's face was blazing. He was frigging euphoric!

'Are you alright? Are you okay?' Allie was fretting over him, helping him down, chastising Sky and stroking her at the same time.

'Jesus, Heath – you gave me a right scare,' I said. 'Are you sure you're okay?'

He didn't even need to answer. The fire in his eyes said it all.

'It was too soon. I shouldn't have let you ride her yet – what the hell was I thinking?' Allie was saying.

Heath put his hand on Allie's shoulder. As if to say, *I'm alright. Stop panicking.*

She pulled Sky towards her, making sure she was

okay too, stroking her and hushing her and reaching out for Heath at the same time.

Frankie arrived.

'You scared the bloody life out of Sky, Frank – yelling like that!' Allie barked.

'Sorreey!' he said. 'I forgot she was a nutcase!'

'She's not a nutcase, Frank, she's just a horse who's been through a lot!' Allie almost screamed at him. 'Thank God Heath handled her well.'

She drew Heath towards her and told him over and over again how he'd done a great job bringing Sky back in.

'You know, your mum always used to talk about horses,' she said to him. 'Not that we saw too many round where we lived – but she had a thing about them. Just like you and Ben seem to have.'

Me? I was included in this? Did I have a 'thing' about them?

'She'd have been proud of you both,' she said, her eyes misting up.

Why the hell would Heath's mum be proud of me? She didn't know me from Adam. Or Eve for that matter. But all of a sudden my chest was hurting. Something was crashing and swelling inside me and I could see *Simon Street* again in a red crayon scrawl. And huge invisible hands scooping me into a white room. What the hell was going on inside my head?

Chapter thirty

The lough seemed to have a really ugly brown lace of muddy water at its edge, which was about all I could see in the fog which had thickened up since earlier in the day. I could smell the water though – all cold and fishy gloom.

It was after lights out now but I couldn't sleep so I'd taken myself off for a walk. I'd disappeared to my room after dinner. I just couldn't face another Circle Time when pieces of a jigsaw were coming together in my head.

I was rigid with questions, aching with – I don't know – confusion. Why hadn't I asked Allie what she meant about Heath's mum? Instead of just taking Sky's reins and leading her back to the stables?

Heath. What did my old life have to do with Heath? Or his mum? I tried to sift particles of information through my brain. Somewhere, someone knew me, knew who my mother was, knew my blood, my bones. What did Heath know? No story is the tale of just one person – or so Mum used to say. Maybe she'd been dropping clues all along.

'What the hell's wrong with *you*?'

It was Frankie. He'd obviously followed me, probably about to go into a rage because I was at *his* bloody cottage. But right now I didn't give a flying frig about Miller's place. I just wanted to get away. To think about the truth – a huge, dark truth that was finally starting to make sense to me.

But Frank wasn't interested in what was going on inside my head.

'You'd better come back,' he said. 'That fog's like soup and it'll soon be pitch dark.'

Flippin' heck – when did Frankie get to be so sensible? But I didn't want to go back. The darkness was falling already but I didn't even care if I got lost.

'Hey, can you hear that, Ben?' Frank said, turning in the direction of the lough.

An outboard motor was thrumming somewhere and muffled voices drawing near. Frank's ears were on red alert.

'Who the frig is it?' he was saying, trying to peer through the mist.

The motor was turned off. Then footsteps, swearing, voices. I couldn't have cared less, but the next thing Frankie slammed me down into the dirt. More muffled voices. Shuffling sounds. I was sure I could feel clouds boiling in across the lough. Bloody hell – all of a sudden I just wanted to be home. *Home* – in Chester Road. I felt sick. Sick about everything.

'Why are we hiding?' I croaked. My throat felt like it was locking. My head was bursting. I just wanted Frankie to piss off.

'*Be quiet!*' Frankie hissed. 'I just had a feeling he'd come back. I *knew* it!'

'Who? What are you on about, Frankie?'

'Wilson. Can't you hear him?'

I could. And Helen Crawford's voice too. What the hell were they up to? We could hear a sort of rattling sound, like something thudding across the ground.

'The jerrycans!' Frankie whispered, wide-eyed. 'They're taking the jerrycans.'

'Taking them away maybe? In the boat?'

'*Shhhh!*'

The rattling and thudding had stopped. Now we could only hear heavy footsteps. The kind of footsteps people lumbering along carrying enormous jerrycans would make.

'They're going up to the house!' Frankie hissed. 'Wilson's sneaking in there sideways and he's gonna do real harm! We have to stop them!'

Who did he think he was? Bruce Willis?

'How the bloody hell can we do that? The Honcho's mad as a cut snake! He might even be armed!'

'Right. But they're lugging jerrycans, and we can run. We can circle round them to get to the house and raise the alarm.' He leapt to his feet.

I jumped up and started to follow him. My chest was pounding with nervous pain.

'*Aow!*'

Frankie swung around. 'What now? Jesus, Ben, come *on*! And keep your bloody voice down!"

'*Aow! Aow! Aow!*' I gasped in a throaty whisper. 'I've twisted my friggin' ankle!' Bloody hell, the pain was searing up my leg.

'Just man up and come *on*!' Frankie roared in a whisper.

'I *can't*!' I croaked. '*You* go!'

He took off like a rocket.

Here I was – supposed to be going home the next day and I was half crippled, blinded by mist, and watching my mate chase off after two wackos who were lugging cans of petrol up to fry the centre. Even on my last evening Knockmore was bloody *unpredictable*!

I hauled myself up and tried to drag my foot behind me across the fields. Shit – it was excruciating. Why couldn't the very last night at this place just be normal? I limped until the muscles in my legs felt like hard rocks.

And then I heard it – the shrill sound of a fire alarm.

Action Man Frankie had saved the day – or the night.

And after that came the commotion! (One of Gran's words.) Screaming and shouting and wailing and madness – the whole place panicking.

And then there was a loud explosion that stopped me in my tracks and I swear I will never forget that sound as long as I live.

I stumbled along until the centre came into view.

Fire was roaring in the hall of the old house and the reception building looked like a glass box of flame.

My heart was pounding in my ears as I raced up to the house, ignoring the pain in my ankle.

Then the Honcho burst out of the reception door in flames. A ball of fire cursing and swearing and crying like a maniac. Flames licking his face like hissing serpents while Chris the Priss battered him with a wet towel. Allie was pushing people out through the fire exit at the side of the building and

Helen Crawford was lying face down on the ground, her body heaving with giant, pulsing sobs.

It was like time stood still. There was chaos all around me but I just felt like I was on the outside, watching a stupid movie or something. I stood there and I couldn't freakin' move. This wasn't happening – this seriously wasn't happening!

'What the feck?' I screamed at Chris, my voice shrieking like an opera singer. *'What was that explosion? What did he do?'*

'He sloshed petrol all around the ground floor!' Chris shouted back. *'He must have turned on the gas in the kitchen to hurry things up. The kitchen door and windows are blown to smithereens! Crazy bastard – he set fire to himself and could have killed us all! It's spread to the main house now!'*

Then I heard Allie screaming, *'Heath! Heath!'* She was pushing through everyone, counting, panicking. She clocked me and I saw a flicker of relief, but she kept looking around wildly. Where the hell *was* Heath? And that's when it got real for me. In a horrible black moment it hit me that Heath was still inside that building. He had one of the rooms in the old bit and he was probably wearing his headphones and hadn't heard a thing. Surely he'd have heard or even felt the explosion? But where was he then?

I ran up to the front door of the old house. The sight of those balls of flame was probably *the* most scary thing I had ever seen in my life. But something made me rush in there like a shark after flesh. Guilt? Maybe. Whatever the reason, I had to play the friggin' hero.

But there was no hope of reaching the staircase to get upstairs. Confronted by flames and smoke, a sharp, black ball of it, I swung around and decided to get myself out of there pronto. Only by now the front door was bloody impassable as a petrol-soaked rug went up in flames and had spread to the big draught-excluder curtains hanging at each side of the door. I ripped my T-shirt off and flapped it at the flames in front of me, making it worse. I couldn't think straight. The heat was scorching my face, the smoke turning the place acrid with sticky stench. The flames were crackling like firelighters in my brain.

'*Help!*' I screamed.

My eyes were stinging and the stink was starting to fill me up inside. The hall was thick with black smoke. I couldn't breathe. I couldn't see. I staggered blindly towards the common-room door but misjudged and ran into a tall bookcase standing to the side of it. The bookcase rocked and something hard and heavy fell from on top of it – a brass ornament – and struck me on the head. I fell to the ground dazed and lay there.

I forced myself to my hands and knees and crawled into the common room. Banging the door closed behind me to stop the fire spreading, I crawled forward. Then I blacked out and when I opened my eyes again, gasping for breath, I could see Heath on the other side of the glass patio door, coming at it with a weapon of some sort. He was beating at the glass. *Bang! Bang! Bang!* I could hear cracking. Glass shattering. Sharp pieces showering on to the floor.

And then he was climbing through and coming to me through the smoke.

Then blackness.

'Ben! Ben! Are you alright?'

Allie's voice was pushing its way like a nail into my brain.

Heath's face was coming closer like a vision. My skin feeling like it didn't belong to me. Then a mouth on mine, blowing, heaving air into mine. Then a head drawing back and eyes searching me.

'Ben! Ben!'

I had never heard Heath shout before. Not ever!

'Ben! Wake up, Ben! Wake up!'

So I drew breath in, inhaled with a rasping howl.

Sick spewed out and I felt so cold, so frigging cold, that my body seemed to weaken and I stopped moving. And I remembered that he'd saved me before. This was not the first time.

My brother had carried me to safety for the second time in his life.

Chapter thirty-one

'Is he awake? Ben? Ben – it's Mum here.'

Lights seemed to be dancing around me – searing lights that were hurting every nerve in my head. There was someone crying – I think. And Dad's voice, all deep and awkward, comforting her.

'Ben? Can you see me? Can you hear me, love?' said Mum.

I could feel her hand on my forehead and smell her warm, soupy breath, coming in waves. But I couldn't answer her. I was just too tired. Maybe she'd wait a while, just hang on a bit till I'd finished my sleep. Deep, deep sleep. Yeah, just for a little while.

'Ben? It's me – Amy. Can you wake up now,

241

please? I really don't like you sleeping this long. Wake up and come and play with me?'

Yeah, in a while, Ames. In a while. Stars seemed to be doing a salsa in my head. Voices all coming at me. Someone saying I hadn't returned to full consciousness yet. My dad was asking when I was going to wake up. I could hear impatience in his voice. Fear even.

'He didn't take too much smoke into his lungs, Mr Parker, thank goodness,' said a heavy voice. 'His lungs are still carrying plenty of oxygen to the brain and the rest of his body. But he *was* concussed and we don't know how long the loss of mental function will last.'

'And if it lasts too long?' my mum was asking.

I didn't hear an answer. Just the sound of Dad's footsteps and a door banging closed. 'Don't be mad, Dad,' I was saying inside my head.

If only they would all just let me sleep. I started drifting away again. Falling into delta waves. Then blackness all around me. Trying to remember my other past, the bit before the beginning. My back story.

Hours, days later, trolley wheels were clanking along corridors, bottles jangling on them. Sing-song voices chatting. Feet were shuffling into my room.

Sky cantering around the field in my imagination.

'Morning, Ben. It's a bright, sunshiny day – come on, love, wake up and let's see those lovely eyes of yours.'

Another voice: 'It's been two days now. I just hope he wakes up soon. His poor family is in pieces.'

More chatter over a clipboard. Sheets being pulled back. A warm sponge rubbing against my legs.

'What on earth did he run into a burning building for?'

'Who knows, Maureen? God only knows what they get up to in that Knockmore place!'

'What time does your shift finish?'

'In about an hour or so. Think I'll take the youngsters to Bangor for the day. Make the most of that weather before the summer's over.'

'*Summer goes, summer goes, like the sand beneath my toes!*'

'Jesus, Maureen – no need to go all poetic on me!'

Laughter, chitchat, getting on with things. These two sounded as happy as pigs in muck. I was on the outside, not watching exactly, but listening. Making no smart comments for a change. I was in limbo – if such a place existed.

'Hello, love. Bit early for visiting,' one of them was saying.

'I know, but – I just wanted to see him,' came a shaky answer. Lauren.

I could smell her, feel her freshness in the room. I wanted to call out, say something to her, say anything, but I was still locked in somehow.

'Hi, Ben. It's me. Just wanted to say hello,' she breathed.

'I'm afraid he won't say much back to you, love. He's Mr Silence, this one.'

'That makes a change!' Lauren laughed quietly. 'You don't mind if I stay with him for a bit?'

'No skin off my nose, love. But the doctor will be around soon and he might shoo you away. But you keep him company till then, pet.'

Maureen and her mate clattered happily away to the next room and Lauren's hand covered mine. Warm and soft like always.

'We did it, Ben – we saved Knockmore,' she whispered. 'The fire brigade arrived in time to save the old house, apart from the damage in the hall – and a mystery benefactor is buying the house from Wilson so all the debts will be covered.' Her voice sounded light, happy. 'Some other benefactors have come up with money for renovation and funding for the future,' she went on. 'And Allie's in charge now. Wilson's been taken away. He's in hospital now but then he'll be locked up somewhere safe.'

I wanted to ask all kinds of questions. Was everybody alright? Where was Heath? Who was looking after the animals? But I couldn't get the words to form.

'I'm going back to school next week,' she was saying. 'Gonna really put my head down and try to get through my exams and stuff. Mum hopes I'll go to Queen's someday like she did. I kinda fancy doing geography.'

I didn't know her mum had gone to university – just assumed she hadn't. But that was the old Ben – Mr Pre-Judge. I wanted her to keep talking. I loved her voice rhyming in my ears. It was way better than those weird humming, buzzing sounds going round and round in my brain. Sounds of numbness and dizziness. But I really wanted to know about my brother.

'Ben, are you in there?' Lauren was saying. 'Do you remember any of it?'

Remember? It was all I could do to summon up enough energy to send blood around my body. To make myself function at some level. My eyelids flickered and I thought I heard a scream.

'Ben, it's okay, we're safe. We're all safe. *Shhhh*.'

Her warm hand on mine again. Had the scream come from me? I could hear fire crackling again. Lights cutting in. My head tried to separate the real from the imaginary.

245

Then I heard another sound. A door opening and closing.

'Ben, Heath's here. He saved you, remember?'

Heath. Heathcliff. Silence. Shuffling feet. Heath's breath as he looked down at me. I could feel him brooding. Struggling to find words. My saviour. My big brother. I don't know exactly when it had come to me, but I knew. I just knew. I could feel him breathing down on me, wondering, working it all out. Did he remember his little brother in that car with him all those years ago? And how did we get separated? Where had he gone when I went to Mum and Dad's? Life leaves trails like tripwires and I felt like I was tripping all over them.

More footsteps. Then a loud voice announcing a name – Doctor Spencer. Another nurse listening.

'Yes, Doctor, I'll raise him up a bit. That might help.'

'Put his arms out over the blankets, Nurse. Let's get him to feel some air.'

'Sorry – do you need us to wait outside?' Lauren was asking.

'No, no, you're fine at the moment. When his parents arrive, however, I'll need some privacy with them.'

'Will he be okay, Doctor?' Lauren's voice again.

'I'm afraid that's something I can only discuss

with his family, but I do have my fingers firmly crossed,' he answered. 'You just keep doing what you're doing and hopefully something will stimulate his brain and bring him back to us.'

He sounded kind, sort of light. Maybe there was hope for me after all?

'And touch his hands, his face – caring touches can provide reassurance and maybe even provoke communication.'

A light laugh. Lauren saying something about 'provoking communication' not being a problem with me before. Before. When *was* before? Before Knockmore? Before almost dying? Before I knew I had a brother?

Then Heath's breath close to my face.

'You want to know what music I listen to?'

In a tone of voice that made it seem like we were back at the beginning of Knockmore and I had only just asked him.

'It's Rag 'n' Bone Man. You wanna listen?'

And he put his headphones on my head.

And there was Rag 'n' Bone Man singing 'Human'.

I listened until Mum and Dad arrived and Heath removed the headphones.

'Ah, Mr and Mrs Parker, I'm glad you're here.' Doctor Spencer again.

Footsteps leaving, footsteps arriving.

Mum clucking round me. Lauren offering to take Amy to the hospital shop while the adults *talked*. Asking Heath to go with her. Doctor Spencer blathering about cognitive impairment, physiological changes. Dad asking the same question over and over again – when was I going to wake up?

'The next day or so is critical, Mr Parker. I *had* hoped he would have regained consciousness by now.'

'Critical? How critical?'

'We're doing a CT scan this afternoon, Mr Parker. I'll be able to tell you more after that.'

'This afternoon? He's been in here for two days! Why wait till this afternoon?'

'Colin, calm down! The doctor's doing all he can.'

And then my father crying. Something I had never heard in over fourteen years of life. Ever! I could hear Mum telling the doctor it was lack of sleep. And then I could feel damp on my face, like a trickle coiling down my cheek. Mum shouting. Dad cursing. The nurse ministering. Doctor Spencer taking charge.

'His eyes are open! His eyes are open!' That was Dad.

Mum's voice calling: *'Ben! Ben!'*

The room a blur of lights and faces and white walls. Mum was crying into my face, begging me, pleading with me to 'come back'. Dad was on my other side, coughing through tears. Then the doc moving them out of the way, fiddling with monitors, giving instructions.

'If you could wait outside for a few minutes?' he said to Mum and Dad.

The nurse was looking into my eyes, talking about the size of my pupils. I felt like I was in a fog. The doctor was asking me to speak but what came out of my mouth was slurred and made no sense. I just wanted to vomit – and that's exactly what I did. All over Doctor Spencer, the nurse, the bed. Everywhere. This was becoming a bit of a habit.

'Well, that was one way to let us know you were back in the land of the living!' the nurse said, laughing, afterwards. 'Don't worry, Ben, it's not uncommon to feel nauseous after a blow to the head.'

'Sorry about the mess,' I muttered to her.

'Ach, never mind, love. The main thing is you gave all the right answers to the questions. Now we know you're compos mentis again!'

Questions? That's right – the doc had asked me all sorts of daft things, like who was the prime minister, how many fingers he was holding up. Real random stuff. Apparently I'd 'passed' so I was now considered sane and on the road to recovery. Jesus, when had I *ever* been sane?

'We'll keep you in for another night, love,' she was saying, folding the fresh bedding tight into the corners. 'Just to keep an eye on you, then you'll be free to go.'

'Go where?' I asked her.

'Home, love. Where else?'

For a second I had been expecting her to say Knockmore. But I realised that was over now. That part of my life was behind me. The doc said I would probably always have a scar where the brass ornament – a bull, I think it was – sliced my head. I didn't care – a scar is a story to tell, just like the one next to my left eye. Proof that Knockmore had happened. Proof that I had met people who would become part of my life. Proof that I'd had an experience that changed me forever.

Chapter thirty-two

So Helen Crawford had known the truth after all. She sent me to Knockmore knowing. Knowing everything. She was out on bail at the minute, Frank said. Charged with a whole litany of offences. Frank had shown me her picture in the paper. White as a ghost. Thin as a spectre. I suppose that's what she would always be for me: a white spirit who did all the wrong things for sometimes the right reasons. She had known my story, known that Heath and I had survived the crash that had killed our parents, known that I was adopted and he wasn't. Had heard Mum talk about me when they worked together – they were 'friends' after all before they became enemies. I could just imagine Mum yapping about my 'foibles' (that's peculiarities to you) – and so Helen had known how to push my buttons. God, she was ruthless. She must have forged that scrap of paper saying *Simon Street*, adding in the crayon scrawl that was supposed to be mine. Or could it have been genuine? In which case, the adult handwriting might have belonged to either one of my original parents. But where would Helen have found such a thing? I shook the thought away – it was too upsetting.

Mum and Dad never met Heathcliff – they were just told that I had an older sibling who was 'too disturbed' to be considered for fostering or adoption. Apart from that, they knew nothing else. You didn't in those days.

Alone, Heath's traumatic experience had driven him inside himself. Lost for years in a shelter of his own making.

Weeks later Allie was sipping coffee in our kitchen. Heath, Mum, Dad, Amy and I were listening to her speaking tentatively. Slowly rolling out the story for us.

'I didn't recognise you at first, Ben,' she was saying. 'It took a while to join the dots and when you told me your name was Eddie Rogan I was afraid of the truth. Afraid of the whole thing tumbling out. Afraid of you hating me. You see, I wasn't in a very good place after your mum and dad died. I should have pulled myself together more quickly. By the time I'd got myself sorted you were gone and Heath seemed to have settled in the care home. Or so I thought. I knew I couldn't dump all my sorrow on him though. He was too ... broken.'

I looked over at my brother, sitting on the edge of our brown sofa, looking lost. For a minute I could feel sharp words jangling in my mouth. How could Allie have abandoned us like that? She was our aunt for God's sake! But I guess she had her scars like the rest of us and the past was the past.

'She was a real reader, your mum,' Allie was saying, smiling to herself. 'She'd get lost for days in some gothic saga and you would hardly get a word out of her.'

Heath and I sort of grinned at each other. It had turned out that neither of us were big readers – so 'Mum' hadn't passed that on to us!

'I told her when each of you was born – I said "Mona, don't do it. You can't give him a name like that – he'll be a laughing stock." 'Allie drank the dregs of her coffee and laughed to herself. 'Heathcliff and Edgar – I mean, you wouldn't, would you?' There was a sort of glint in her eye. Like she was being cheeky and disrespectful.

'*Edgar?* She called me *Edgar*?' I squeaked. Yep, the squeak was back!

'Yes. Both characters out of *Wuthering Heights*,' Allie answered. 'God, she loved that book!'

Bloody hell! I would *not* be telling anyone else that I was called Edgar! Thank God for 'Ben Parker'!

'So, where do we go from here?' Mum asked, lifting her mug shakily to her lips.

My 'real' mum – the mum I had grown up with. My mum who had been hurt over and over again … until she had me.

And Amy.

At Mum's question Amy looked at me with something like fear in her eyes and I thought I heard a faint discharge of breath, like she'd been holding it in.

'Well, I'm not going anywhere, Mum,' I said. 'I'm home, and I'm here to stay.'

Her eyes started welling up and Dad turned his head away in case I might catch his emotion. Dad and emotion weren't two things you normally put in the same sentence – until Knockmore, that is.

'Heath?' I said. 'What about you?'

For a long moment he stared at me and I thought he was going back to his wall of silence. His place of refuge.

Mum grazed his arm with her hand and willed

him to speak. Then she decided to go first.

'Heath, I'm sorry you and Ben were separated. I didn't know – I didn't know to fight for you too. I know it's too late now, but … would you like to try us out? We're not perfect – in fact, we're far from perfect, but there's room at the inn.' She laughed, a brittle sound. 'And if you'd like to – we could give it a go?'

My big brother looked at me long and hard. He looked through me and beyond me even. I could only guess at what those eyes had seen so long ago. Just a few years older than me and yet he must have pulled me to safety.

'Did you know me, Heath?' I asked. 'When I first came to Knockmore?'

He shook his head. Closed his eyes for just a minute. Then he said: 'We were in the back seat. Your wee hands had grabbed my comic off me and I was shouting at you. Mum was telling me to stop. To stop shouting … to stop talking.'

He was barely audible now. I could feel something tighten in my chest. I felt clammy all of a sudden – my palms were sweating.

'Dad turned round too,' he went on. 'He took his eyes off the road. Just for a second, I swear! Just for a second! And that's all I remember. Apart from saving *you*.' He was sobbing now, streams of tears spilling down his face. 'But I did as Mum asked. I stopped talking.'

So silence became his safe place. My heart felt like it was swelling up, taking up space so my lungs couldn't expand and my limbs couldn't move.

'I guess Helen Crawford did us a favour, Mum,' I said, using what felt like a lungful of breath.

'She did, son, but she certainly didn't intend to. We know she was trying to help Wilson and Knockmore ... but maybe that wasn't her only motive.' Mum set her mug down again. 'She obviously discovered that Allie was related to your mum – so maybe she was trying to drive a wedge between you and us – your adoptive parents. We'll never know, but the important thing is you three have found each other now.' She looked around at each of us. 'It's a lot for you all to take in ... it will take a while.'

Her eyes had clouded up again and I knew this was hard on her. And Dad.

Amy on the other hand was watching Heath with wonder – like he was the most exotic reptile she'd ever seen.

'Wanna see my tarantula, Heath?' she asked him.

He studied her like he'd never seen anything like her. Then his face actually broke into a smile, a lopsided smile that made him look young, like a teenager. Like he was supposed to be.

'Yeah,' he said. Almost inaudibly. 'Go on then.'

She took him by the hand – by the *hand*! – and led him to the weird and wonderful place that was Amy's world. If Heath was ever going to make a decision about staying with my wacko family – this was the crucial point.

'Ben's alright – sometimes,' she was telling him as they climbed the stairs. 'He thinks he's all mean and moody but he's a bit of a wuss really. Don't tell him that though.'

I had to laugh. And Mum laughed and Dad laughed and even Aunt Allie laughed.

'Your dad was a bit like you,' Allie said. 'A real rebel without a cause. But he'd be proud of you boys. I know he would.'

'Do I look like him?'

'You look like your mum,' she answered. 'The same speckled eyes. She and I both had them.'

The song-thrush eyes. I noticed them the first time I saw her. I thought it was weird that someone else – other than me – had brown 'measles' in their eyes. The clues had been there all along. Heath had them too, but because he never looked you straight in the eye, I just hadn't noticed them.

'But you've got your dad's personality,' she went on. 'I was sad about them for a long, long time, Ben.

But there's a new future now – with you and Heath and this lovely family.' She nodded shyly at my *real* mum and dad.

'Will you keep working at Knockmore?' I asked her.

'God, yes! Knockmore gives me a reason to get up every day. It always has. Chris and I … well, we'd like to turn the place around. Keep on giving youngsters the time out they need.'

'So you'll have a whole new bunch soon to drive you crazy?' I laughed.

'Well, maybe not as crazy as you lot. Definitely not as crazy as Frank!' she laughed, blowing her fringe away yet again. 'But it'll be a challenge. And I hope they can find something in Knockmore that will help them to heal. Will you keep in touch with Lauren?'

'Yeah. Course.'

I was blushing – I know I was. The thought of going back to Simon Street to see her made me all sort of fluttery and jittery. Not just seeing Lauren – but the place itself. It was where I had lived before the crash. It was where I had come from. I couldn't help thinking life would have been so different – not better, not worse, just different.

'And that chip on your shoulder?' Allie asked, smiling. 'Is it gone?'

'Let's just say it's more of a French fry these days than a chunky chip,' I mumbled.

The truth was, I had nothing to be resentful about. I had a family and friends that were all pretty okay. And I *thought* I had turned one of those corners they were always going on about at Knockmore. I wouldn't say I was 'fixed' but I was as good as I was gonna get. Until –

'Mum! My tarantula's escaped!'

Mum rolled her eyes and nodded at me.

'Ben, go and help her find it, love, will you?'

'Seriously, Mum? You want *me* to save her tarantula?'

Mum nodded. An affirming nod that sort of said Sindy the Corn Snake was forgotten.

So I clambered up the stairs two at a time and yeah – you guessed it – I landed full smack on top of Talula the freakin' Tarantula. She crunched and squelched under my Size 7 foot and I thought – bloody great – here we go again!

Amy screamed, Mum yelled up the stairs and Dad groaned . . . and I reckoned I'd be back in Knockmore before you could say 'Chris the Priss!'

Heath just looked at us all as if we were as mad as a box of frogs.

'Welcome to the family, mate,' I said, feeling like crap.

And then he did something really strange. He raised his hand and put it up against mine. Like a bridge. And I saw that his fingers were the same as mine, solid as walls. And the same map of lines ran through his palm, telling the same family story. I knew I'd probably never know the whole story – not completely. But I had enough for now and I was guessing that Heath had too.

We tried to gather up what was left of Talula and to persuade our little sister that we weren't psychopathic animal-killers.

And crossed our fingers and hoped that Mum wouldn't be filling out *another* application form for Knockmore!

Which actually wouldn't be such a bad thing – at least I'd get to see Sky again.

The End

If you enjoyed this book from
Poolbeg why not visit our website

www.poolbeg.com

and get another book delivered straight
to your home or to a friend's home.

All books despatched within 24 hours.

Free postage on orders over €20*

Why not join our mailing list at
www.poolbeg.com and get some
fantastic offers, competitions,
author interviews, new releases
and much more?

 @PoolbegBooks

www.facebook.com/poolbegpress

*Free postage over €20 applies to Ireland only